Subterranea

Copyright 2012 © Mary Hahn
First Edition

This is a work of fiction. Names, characters, businesses, places, events and incidents are either the products of the author's imagination or used in a fictitious manner. Any resemblance to actual persons, living or dead, or actual events is purely coincidental.

ISBN-13: 978-1479233625

Mary Hahn

Subterranea

❦

Book 1

For Cian, who said it was his favorite book.

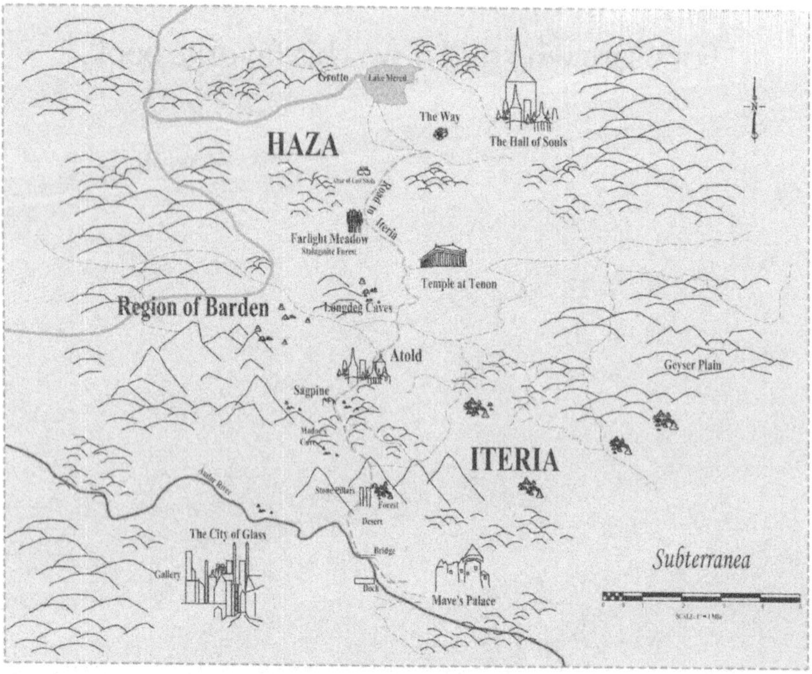
Grotto
Lake Merell
The Way
The Hall of Souls
HAZA
Road to Iteria
Farlight Meadow
Stalagmite Forest
Temple at Tenon
Region of Barden
Longdeg Caves
Atold
Geyser Plain
Sagpine
ITERIA
Stone Pillars
Forest
Desert
The City of Glass
Gallery
Bridge
Dock
Mave's Palace
Subterranea

PART I

· ONE ·

Annah sang softly. "Storybook, storybook, where are you? Hiding here your leaves of gold. Pages crumbled, wise, and old..." The words she had recently made up, but the melody had always been with her. When the haunting melody had first crept into her thoughts it had frightened her because she was so small, and because she didn't know how it had found her. But after years of humming it, setting it to words, it became familiar, like a lullaby learned in a mother's arms or a game-rhyme picked up from a friend. She hoped she had first heard the song in her mother's arms.

Then it would be more than a song. It would be a gift from the mother she had never known.

    Annah bent over the large toy box in the Children's Playroom. Her hand poked around in the wooden box until she found the book she was looking for. "There you are," she said. Her fingers grasped the soft leather cover. She tucked the book under her arm next to Abbi, her doll. "What story shall I read to the children today?" she asked, smoothing the doll's torn lace apron.

    She was 14 now, too old to play with dolls. But Abbi had been with her all these years, proof that she had once lived in a real home before coming to Seton House.

    Then something in the toy box caught her eye. Squinting into the jumble of toys and books she saw a flicker of light. She pushed the things aside and discovered a gaping hole in the bottom of the toy box. The hole extended through the floor that had rotted away, revealing a dark place, which she supposed must be a boiler room or forgotten basement. How many toys have fallen through? She wondered in dismay.

She peered into the hole and saw a blue light a few feet down, a pastel sheet hovering in space. Through and beyond the misty blue was dark that went on forever, like a starless night sky. She thrust her hand into the hole and felt the rush of cold air. Her hand stretched out to the sides and found walls—not of plaster, but of damp rock, like the mussel-matted boulders of the seashore. She could not reach the blue light.

"What an odd, secret place," she said.

Secrets. She had often walked the halls of Seton House, looking for doors, passageways to those secret places of her dreams—cottages filled with sunlight and flowers and family. She had discovered secrets all right, night secrets, in the form of sounds: the scratching of branches on windows where no trees grew, the wailing of the wind on windless nights. On these nights she imagined fairies came to spread enchantment, and in the morning Seton House never seemed as dreary.

But that was pretend. There were no secret places, only wishes that never came true.

Bending at the waist, she poked her head deep into the tunnel through the bottom of the box. She expected to see lost books and toys scattered on a lower floor.

The sheet of light lay within reach now. Her fingers grazed the blue mist and she watched as her nails became blue-tipped.

Then she noticed something that was not there a moment ago. Past the light was, of all things, a flower, and it was the most beautiful flower she had ever seen. Its scarlet trumpet held an egg-sized blue crystal that was the source of the light. It appeared to be floating in space, but Annah figured it was attached, perhaps even growing, on the rocky wall that she could feel but not see.

She gasped when she saw the stone. It must be worth a fortune! Bending forward, she stretched her head into the blue light and thrust out her hand to grasp the crystal. She could not reach it. She could not move forward another inch. And to her horror she could not pull out. Her shoulders were trapped in the opening, and the cold rocky walls seemed to close in on her. The slightest movement brought pain as the rocks tore across her upper arms.

"Help," she groaned. "I'm stuck. Headmistress Downing!"

Silence. Terrible silence.

"He-ya," someone whispered. The voice came from the darkness below.

Annah's eyes widened. "Who's there?"

"Eelin," said the quiet, careful voice. There was something odd about the voice, something gravelly and animal-like.

"Eee-lin?" Annah twisted her shoulders in the cramped space. "Stuck," she moaned. She stared desperately at the blue stone and wiggled her outstretched fingers at it which brought pain to her shoulders and neck.

A warm, bristly hand clamped around hers and began to pull her down.

"No!" she yelled. "Push me back! Push me back inside the toy box!"

The tugging on her hand stopped. "What is your name?"

"My name? Annah."

"Annah," the voice said gently. "Come with me."

In one swift motion, the hand pulled Annah through the toy box, through the tunnel.

Wet cold stung her face. "Stop!" she begged. "I don't want to go." But through the blue mist she was pulled, past the velvety flower with its dazzling crystal that followed her like a living, all-seeing eye.

She landed flat on her back, on damp ground. Around her spun a murky place which reeked of mold and rot, and of burning embers, and of something tangy she could not identify. She rubbed her eyes and they began to tear.

She kept still while her eyes adjusted and the room steadied. Next to her lay the book and doll she had forgotten she was holding. She gathered her things, held them close, and looked around at the sunless cavern. She knew in an instant she had fallen into a foreign world. She had found her secret place all right. But this was nothing like the places of her dreams.

A shadowy creature loomed toward her. A clawed hand reached out, and then a face appeared in the blue light. It grinned, showing huge teeth.

Annah screamed and scooted backward through the dirt until a stone wall stopped her. She stared at the hideous creature that had jumped back at her scream but who now approached her cautiously. It stopped a few inches from her and stared back at her with cocked head.

It was a hairy, large-boned monster with a flattened sausage for a nose, pointed ears, and huge, shifting, wild eyes. The hair was a good foot longer than her own, hair that had probably never been cut, blue-black and divided into a dozen braids woven with gold threads.

It was a male, she supposed, for he wore heavy trousers and a pale shirt made of fine cloth. He was dressed like any boy you might see on the street, but he wore no shoes. And what shoes would fit his square feet? The thick toenails curled upward and were filed to sharp points.

Around his waist he wore a wide leather belt, slung low on one side, with pouches hanging from it. He wore an iron scabbard inlaid with rubies. The rubies were the size of thumbnails.

The creature studied her for a long while, looking at every inch of her, looking inside her, she thought. He reached up and stroked the tongued petals of the flower on the cavern wall where the light still bloomed in the crystal. The creature stepped forward and made a move for Annah's head, in a petting way.

Annah raised her mouth to the fissure overhead and screamed, "Help me!" Her voice made a hollow, empty-church sound. Tears streamed down her cheeks. "Please," she whispered.

The creature grunted. "Come," he commanded in a stern voice. He reached down and took her arm and began to pull her toward a darksome passageway.

Annah struggled to break free, but her forearm was held steadfast in the creature's clamp. She kicked him and clawed at his face. He didn't pull back. "What's the matter with you, you filthy beast?" she shouted. His body seemed oblivious to pain, to touch.

"Please let me go," she cried as she was pulled through the gloomy tunnel. But in her heart she knew that all the pleading in the world wouldn't help. She knew what this creature must be. A troll.

She had heard the midnight stories, scary tales told by lonely dormitory girls. She had only half-believed the stories, and at any rate thought she was safe, for trolls were trapped miles beneath the earth, deprived forever of sky and trees and sunlight. They were related to humans, it was said, born of the same primeval parents, but cast underground, where they had evolved into something neither human nor beast. In the back of her mind Annah suppressed the knowledge that trolls were known to eat humans. Only a legend, she told herself, a story meant to frighten children. This troll was unlike the trolls of the legends. He was not a slobbery giant with twelve heads. He was near her height, and similar to humans in build, though large-boned. And he did not seem old, for he moved with energy and ease.

"I mean you no harm troll," Annah whispered thickly. She glanced back at the blue light, a star in this dark, terrifying night, and concentrated on the crystal that sparkled with life. She made a wish that it could help her.

"Haza," the troll said in a gruff voice. "You have found Haza."

"Haza?" Annah repeated. She tried to smile, to show him that she was his friend.

He snorted and squeezed her arm. "It means Fire World. Sunless. Fire is our sun."

"Yes," she said. "And you are a troll, aren't you?" She didn't wait for him to answer. "Listen, troll, we come from the same…"

He silenced her with a snort.

Soon they came to what Annah supposed was a fork in the tunnel because the troll paused momentarily. Then, without warning, he spun off the path and veered to the right, pulling hard on Annah's arm.

This was the bleakest nightmare Annah could possibly imagine. If only it weren't so dark, and so hard to breathe. The air was ripe with smoke and hot with fire. How her eyes hurt! What in heaven's name were they burning? And the tunnel with its endless drip, drip of water punctuated by the chink of hammers on metal was enough to make her lose her mind.

"You have found Haza and now we go to the Altar," the troll said abruptly.

"Altar?"

"The Altar of Lost Souls," he muttered. "Soulless, do you hear me?"

"But…"

"Enough!"

Annah felt the life drain from her as the hideous creature dragged her deep into the darkest chasms, descending through layers of filthy, ever darker, ever more silent corridors, away from the blue light, far from the toy box and the human world.

· TWO ·

Eelin bowed before the Altar of Lost Souls. He had never been to the sacrificial chamber, this secret hallowed knot in the string of tunnels. For reasons he could not understand he was overcome with feelings of dread the moment he entered the room.

    The chamber with its chalky walls and sagging ceiling was uncomfortably small for a sanctuary, and it smelled of rancor and death. The walls had been decorated with precious stones and small symbols. The brown-green symbols were records marking each sacrifice to the gods. They were too numerous to count.

In the center of the chamber stood a perfectly round, flat stone, stained with the dark blood of sacrifices.

The moment Eelin saw the stone he could hear the screams of humans begging for their lives. He heard the slash of nicon to throats and the tearing of flesh. He saw blood trickle to the floor as his own perspiration ran in rivulets down his forehead, down his chin. Blood, blood, everywhere.

Looking down from its place on the wall stood a bust of Roex, god of good water, and it too was splattered with old blood. Eelin glanced up at the colorless eyes that watched him to make sure he completed his task. He said a silent prayer to the god, seeking to be one with him and receive his strength.

Eelin had imagined he would kill the human right away, to get it over with, and he would kill her, soon. He had no idea how much the human would struggle, how tired he would be from her struggle.

He had formed no ideas about the human at all, really. "At least I should know what the human feels before I silence those feelings," he told himself. "And then I will know my own truth about humans, instead of what others have told me."

He loosened his grip on the girl's arm. She leaned back, exhausted and shaking, against the crumbling wall. She clutched her book to her chest like a shield as though to protect the doll behind it. Eelin knew about books. And dolls too, for that matter.

He smirked, baring his teeth. "I could kill you if I wanted to, you know." This was not what he'd meant to say at all. What he'd meant to say was, "I'm going to kill you." The words he spoke sent a memory rushing back. He remembered what his father had said just before Annah came through the passageway:

"I am tired of waiting for the human to come forth," Rud muttered. "At this rate it might be seasons before the human is killed and Loge's death is avenged. The humans took our precious stones. In return for their plagues. Half of Haza lost to their filth." He looked sternly at Eelin. "Once the human comes and the Way is closed, no more of them will taint

Haza. No trace of their foul blood will remain. Not even a memory!"

"And Loge's death…"

"Revenge will be served." Rud fingered his necklace and sliced his thumb on one of the human teeth that had been honed to sharp points. He put his thumb to his mouth and sucked the purplish blood. He closed his eyes.

"Young Loge, his body on the pallet, ablaze in orange flames. Did you know, Second Son, that the pallet, when it first took fire, began to rock to and fro like a cradle…" He snorted, and his hands curled into fists. "The foul-smelling human must be killed in the proper manner and in the proper place. And it must be killed by you, Second Son." He paused. "When the Way closes I can die in peace," he murmured. "I have commissioned burial leathers. I am ready to sleep, ready to step down from the Chair of Light."

"Yes, Father."

"You do want to be king, don't you?" he had asked Eelin.

"With my soul," Eelin had answered, kneeling down to kiss the sword that his father held out.

"Esauit." Eelin felt pleasure. Only trolls of royal blood possessed a soul; all others were lost.

Rud had smiled. "Kill it, finish it. And bring me its teeth."

"Yes, my Lord."

The girl's body stiffened. "Please don't, I beg of you," she said, blindly directing her words to the tree root grazing his cheek. "I was only looking for my book." Tears shone in her eyes, and her face was smeared with dirt. "Is that why you pulled me in? To kill me?" she asked.

Eelin was taken aback. "I pulled you in because," he answered gruffly, "you found Haza." He had never imagined the human to be so bold with its questions. A human, Rud always said, was dumb as a crawler, and just as filthy. A human was foul to look upon. But then Rud hated humans.

"But I didn't ask to come here to this, this Haza. You could have pushed me back," the girl said. "You could have."

"I was commanded by Rud..." he stammered.

"I'm just a child. You can tell Rud..."

"You are human. Hqim," he said, in the ancient tongue.

"Yes, I am human. Is that wrong?" Her voice took on a proud edge.

He sighed. "If it makes you feel better, it wasn't always this way. Many seasons ago, before my birth, we traded wisdom. The humans gave us words. And," he added, "disease." He regretted saying the words as soon as they came from his lips. *I speak too much*, he scolded himself.

She began to cry, her shoulders heaving.

How strongly the human clings to life, Eelin thought. How odd that she shows both her proud and pitiful side. Is this a form of human cunning, to show both sides? Does she seek to confuse me? The idea intrigued him. *She* intrigued him. His hand went to his necklace of onyx and diamond. "Rud, my father, commanded me to kill the human when it came through the Way," he found himself saying. "Red blood mixed with the blue blood of the crystal. The crystal dies. The passageway closes." He was stalling now, he knew it.

"Passageway? The toy box..." she said softly.

"The last passageway, the last crystal," Eelin said in a voice so sad it surprised him. "And when the Way closes, well, that is the last." The finality of the words filled him with confusion. He could see killing the human—he understood why that must be done—to avenge his brother Loge's death. But closing the Way forever? It meant trolls could never know the human world. It seemed more a punishment for trolls than for humans. Perhaps if he had known Loge things would be different. He would feel Rud's anger. He sighed. Why *this* human? And why couldn't the human have been loud, and noisome, and ugly?

Eelin looked at the stone altar tattooed with brown blood. He pictured himself tearing at this girl, this Annah's skin, white bone exposed, and it made a dull pain start in his chest. He had never killed anything except small prey for food.

Death hung everywhere in this steamy room, the odor sickly sweet, so thick in the air he choked as he pictured human after human thrown upon the altar and slashed to ribbons. Not here, he told himself. I will kill her, but not here, where so many have been slaughtered.

"We must go to another place," Eelin said abruptly, turning his back on the altar.

"Please," she said. Her warm breath brushed his ear. "I want to go home."

"Not possible," he snapped. He pulled sharply on her arm, leading her uphill through the musty corridor, toward a wider channel. The sacrificial room was too hot anyway, he told himself. Death and gods, gods and death. The two should never come together, never be mentioned in the same breath. He glanced back at the altar standing perfectly round in the crooked room. He was glad to leave it behind.

༄༅

For nearly half a rotation they traveled in darkness, or so it was for Annah, Eelin knew. But he could see as though the cave were lit by a thousand torches. Seeing in the dark was no feat; if only he could see in sunlight.

Many thoughts whirled in his head as he looked at Annah. After Rud had placed the crystal in the flower, the Saqa, Eelin had come many times to the rocky crevice to wait, and to watch. He had seen the human fingertips graze the blue light. He had picked up the books and play-trinkets that littered the ground, things that had fallen through when the hole was first made. He hid the human relics in the bottom of the garment chest in his chamber. How odd the trinkets were. How extraordinary the books. "A pity I cannot read," he had whispered as his fingers slid across the letters on the smooth paper.

For many rotations he had stared at the blue light, possessed by its power. He had waited impatiently for the human face, but it had not shown itself. Now at last, in the dark, he could look on the face all he wanted. And she could not see him.

He studied her pink mouth, half open as she made her way blindly through the tunnel. How different humans were from trolls! He had never imagined them to look like this.

The girl's teeth were small and dull-tipped and useless. Her eyes were not the color of dampened earth, but of a color he did not recognize. Her body was without wiry black hair, her limbs were long and delicate, and her skin resembled the palest royal moth silk. Her voice was high and smooth, not the low, throaty sound he was used to. And her hair! It was a color he had never imagined hair could be. He wasn't sure, but he thought her hair might be the color of human sunset.

He had never seen sunset, or the sun, for that matter. But he had heard stories. The sun was bad for trolls. It would cause blindness followed by slow, painful death. This was well documented in the Legends of Tye.

How could something wondrous be bad? Eelin had always asked himself. He was not the only troll who asked. The Chronicler did not believe Tye Legend. She told stories of the human sun's beauty, of its miraculous power to light many worlds that floated around it. She said there was even a way for trolls to walk in the human world! And she told stories of fiery sunsets and vast oceans the color of aquamarine, instead of black like Lake Mered. Eelin did not know this human color of ocean. But now, looking at Annah's hair, he thought he knew the color of sunset.

"Do you know sunset?" he asked abruptly, stopping to face her.

"I know a lot of things," Annah said.

"Read, do you?" Eelin asked, touching the book she held.

"Yes, I read, don't you?"

"No," he replied. "But I know the wisdom of the Legends. And I am learning the ancient tongue."

"The Legends?" She held up the book. "Adventures on the High Seas," she said slowly. "It, too, is a legend. And this is a ship. I could teach you," she said, her voice brighter. "I could teach you many things. You could use me..."

Eelin traced the outline of the ship. "I do know ships," he said. "I heard a story once about a ship that sailed for many years without coming to rest, searching, but never finding land." He looked into Annah's eyes. "Are your eyes the color of ocean?"

Annah looked down. "I suppose so."

Eelin nodded. "And mine are the color of dirt." He thought of the legends, not of Tye, but of the Chronicler. The Chronicler claimed to know the truth about humans. That they were good. "And what is The Truth?" he whispered, feeling confused and weak. "We must go now."

With Annah's arm still in his grasp he began to walk, though he slowed his pace so she could rest. He felt her arm go slack in his grip. Does she no longer fear me, or is she dying? he wondered. This made him uneasy. He did not want her to die yet. What is wrong with me that I have not killed her? The question sank like iron in his stomach.

Father wants me to bring back the girl's teeth, he thought. The teeth are so small.

He watched her eyes blinking wildly, as though it could help her see in the dark hall. The clothing she wore, spattered with mud, was decorated with tiny, insignificant flowers. The boots on her small feet were worn, and covered with a paint to hide the cracks in them.

His hand grazed her hair softly so she would not sense his touch. The hair was fluid like water, and softer than feather. She is the color of sunset and ocean, he thought, and I must kill her. Because killing her is the only way to sit on the Chair of Light.

"By doing this task," his father had said in a voice without emotion, as though he were talking about killing a rabbit, "you will pass into the Age of Wisdom. And then you will sit on the Chair."

Eelin grimaced as he remembered his father's words. "It is only a human," he murmured, trying to convince himself. So easily could I kill her, he thought. My brother Mars would surely have killed the girl by now. Killed her and eaten her, and enjoyed it. By now the last crystal would have turned to dust and closed the Way forever. But I am not my brother, and thank the gods for it, he thought.

And Rud, he thinks killing her will prove my strength, prove that I am worthy to rule. "Killing will prove my cruelty," he whispered.

Eelin pictured himself wearing a necklace of Annah's teeth, filed sharp, tiny white daggers. A terrible thought raced through him. Perhaps I <u>am</u> too weak to rule. "I will be king," he promised himself. "I will. "Gstull," he said to keep the words strong.

Eelin blinked when the tunnel opened to the vast stalagmite meadow of phosphorescent light. His eyes were highly sensitive to their pastel glow. The air took a sudden chill from the water seepage overhead. It came in steady droplets, and in earth colors, dark and bland; not really colors at all.

Eelin stopped and released Annah's arm. He raised his nostrils to the air and caught the tart aroma of burning steel.

The girl gasped. An expression of relief crossed her face. "I can see." She looked around slowly, blinking her eyes as though to capture each particle of light. Her gaze stopped at Eelin, and he felt momentarily dizzy, and powerless. "What is this place? It's like a garden full of rainbow chalk." She rested her palm on a pale green spike jutting out of the ground. Eelin thought he saw a smile begin on the girl's face and he looked away.

"Stalagmites," Eelin replied. "I believe they are the souls of the dead seeking light, seeking the human world that was denied them. We are related to humans, you know. Cousins." His words hit him like a blade to the skull. We are related in more ways than language, he thought.

Annah pulled her hand away from the stalagmite and wiped it across her billowy dress. "This is a graveyard?"

Eelin sighed. "Royal graveyard," he replied. "My brother is here. Not his bones, but his soul." He swept the sad thoughts aside. "I am bound by my father to bring back your teeth," he heard himself say, and his voice did not sound like his own. "To prove that you are dead. To avenge my brother's death. By you. You—human."

Annah's eyes grew wide and watery, and she began to scream. She was tired, it was obvious, because her scream was weak. "I haven't killed anyone," she whimpered.

"Silence!" Eelin said. To his amazement she quieted down. An idea struck him. What if I brought Rud back a lock of her hair instead? Rud would believe I've killed the girl, would he not? I could study this creature, this human. And then later, well, we will see.

Without further thought he reached out and grabbed a fistful of Annah's hair and brought it to his lips. It smelled of new life. He opened his mouth and bit off a cluster as easily as though cutting a tender cinvaellis shoot in the phosphorescent canyon.

"You are cruel!" Annah cried. Her hands clutched at her hair and she began to back away, bumping into the stalagmites that covered the floor of the cavern. Some of the stalagmites broke under her boots.

A crunching sound came to Eelin's ears. He was not used to this noise; the leathery pads of his feet were silent when he walked. He brushed the lock of Annah's hair across his fat palm. "Don't worry," he said placidly. He tucked the hair into the smallest leather pouch hanging from his belt. "Perhaps the hair will be enough to convince my father."

She seemed relieved at his words and stopped walking.

He moved close to her, looked her over, and his eyes came to rest on the doll she carried. It was a large, well-worn female doll with a white face, hands, and feet. The amber hair was tightly curled, and wiry like his own. The pale glass eyes were encircled by stiff black hairs.

He had another idea. He touched the doll's hand, surprised at how cold and hard it was, like marble. "I wonder," he said, turning the hand over in his. "I wonder if the fingers would do?"

Eelin lifted the doll's hand to his mouth, and before Annah could say anything he bit, snapping off the two longest fingers. The fingers were indeed stone, and left a fine grit on his thick brown tongue.

"No!" Annah cried. She pulled the doll away and hugged it. The feet swung in the air and touched, sounding like the chink of glass to glass. "Stay away from me, I hate you!" she told him.

Eelin lay the doll fingers out in his palm. They were of human color, though small.

Perhaps Rud would not notice the small size. Everything looked small to Rud because he was so large. Could the fingers fool Rud? Eelin's heart raced at the cleverness of the idea. To claim the Chair without killing the girl? Is it possible?

Annah jerked her dress around her and turned her back to him. She picked her way through the pale shafts that studded the meadow.

She will be safe enough here in Far Light, Eelin thought. "I must go now," he told Annah. "Perhaps if you are obedient I might find a way to send you home." He hoped this would keep her from doing anything foolish like running away.

She stopped walking and said, with her back still to him, "I will find my own way home." She kicked at the ground with the toe of her boot, and a fine green mist rose up around her, sparkling in the light.

"Suit yourself," he said dryly, "but if you leave this meadow, you won't get far before a troll finds you and eats you."

Annah twisted around, wiping the tears from her chin with her palm. "How do I know you won't eat me?"

He snorted. "If I did, I would at least kill you first." He paused. "Do you have any idea how much trouble you..." But he didn't finish. She wouldn't understand. Without further thought, he started toward the dark tunnel that led back to the passageway and grotto. "I will return before two rotations," he said wearily.

"Rotation?"

"Rotation," he called, without looking back. His words echoed off the cavern walls, deepening in pitch upon their return.

"How long is that?" she asked.

"Rotation. Two human hours. Stay here. Stay here, Annah." And he lumbered away, certain that she did not hear the last words he whispered, words that surprised and frightened him: "I cannot kill you."

· THREE ·

"I must seal the Way..." Eelin muttered as he stole through the musty channel. "Before anyone finds out. And I'll need some fresh blood. Oh, why didn't I think of that sooner?" he lamented. "Because I hadn't known in my heart that I wouldn't kill her until I saw her face." The truth frightened him. "I am weak," he told himself. Yet he felt relief. Or was it just pity for the human? He could not answer that question.

He would need to encounter a small animal soon, for its blood, as the Hall was only a short distance away. Already he could hear the voice of the city—the low-pitched hum of words, the whine of music, the growl of sacred cats.

He scanned the tunnel walls, and the roots overhead, and watched for signs of movement. His sharp eyes could detect the slightest twitch of a root many arm's length away. A mawl or other creature was all he needed, really, for the blood. Just a small amount of blood to smear on his face and clothes. "It will help with the lie," he reassured himself.

It was not until he reached the fork in the tunnel that he saw something.

On the ground some feet off a dungrat scurried into a burrow. Eelin loped toward the hole and pounced. He jabbed his arm into the dark hole and withdrew the vermin by its neck. The dungrat hung lifeless in Eelin's grip, its neck broken. It was a tiny animal, no larger than a young bat.

He knew he would have to be conservative with the blood. He bit the neck, drained the blood, and smeared it on his face, his hands, and across the front of his shirt. He took the doll fingers from the pouch and rolled the fingers in blood and dried them with warm breath before putting the fingers back. Then he swallowed the animal in one gulp.

"There," he said, wiping his mouth on his sleeve, "that part is done."

As he followed the worn path toward the grotto he began to think about Annah. *I hope she will stay in Far Light until I return. If I return.*

A terrible thought kept surfacing: *what if Rud does not believe me and sends Mars to finish what I could not?* He tugged at his black braids nervously. *I should have left her with someone who could hide and protect her. Father will simply have to believe me. That is all there is to it.*

Eelin did not let himself think about the grave punishment he would receive if his father found out he was lying. All he could think about was Annah. "Strange I should care so much for the human," he said. "But if I do not protect her, who will?"

The tunnel widened just past the fork. He swung to the left, watching anxiously for the passageway. At last the cavern opened wider and he saw the rocky alcove where Annah had come through. He hastened toward it when he found the faint blue light still glowing in the opening. He half expected to see his father waiting there for him. "How lucky I am," he whispered. "The gods are on my side. It was meant to be."

He stood for some time looking up at the crevice, watching the flower. He put a trembling hand near the light and tried to peer beyond it, to catch a glimpse of what the human world was like. "If only I could see the sky, the sun," he said.

He pictured Annah's hair, yellow mixed with scarlet, brushing softly against the umber cave wall. "If the human dies and the stone dissolves, I will never see sunset. Sqii," he said, in the ancient tongue. "No troll will ever see sunset." The words set his blood pounding through his veins.

Looking at the crystal, he went over in his mind what he must do. If I am to make Rud believe that I have killed the girl, I must complete the lie and close the passageway. I must kill the flower and take the stone.

Eelin reached up and dislodged the crystal from the flower. He watched the rock glow in his hand, felt its solid weight for its size. "What substance is this that it is so heavy?" he breathed. He peered into the stone's center, at the pulsating light, the fire burning in its heart. He felt as though he held in his hand a thousand leagues of wisdom, a world of secrets, and a magic he could never understand. Carefully he slipped the precious crystal into his trouser pocket. His pocket glowed with a soft blue light that quickly faded.

He reached up and grasped the plant and its roots, tore it from the wall, threw it to the ground, and crushed it with his foot. The petals changed from rich scarlet to dull brown. He picked up the broken flower and examined it closely. Nestled inside the core was a pale seed, hard as the crystal itself. He removed the tiny oval seed and dropped it into the same yellow pouch that contained the lock of Annah's hair.

The moment the crystal was taken from the flower the passageway began to close as though a rock was being rolled across it. The round light from the human world soon became a shard that snapped shut, like an eye closing, leaving the alcove dark and silent.

Eelin looked down, picked up a hard white stone and began to crush it against the cave wall. He pulverized it and sprinkled the salt-sized particles over the damp ground, to mimic the death of the crystal. "This will prove to Father that it is done," Eelin whispered. "Done," he repeated, glancing at the place where the flower had grown. "Later I will figure out a way to reopen it," he whispered.

There came the wail of a lyre and then the drums. Eelin looked to the grotto and saw the yellow torches that burned there, the center of Haza. Voices droning in song reached his ears. The city was celebrating, he remembered. It was Mars's birthday. A hundred and fifteen seasons old.

A sharp pain to his gut brought another memory. Today was the anniversary of his mother's death.

"Where did Hela go?" young Eelin had asked his father. Tears had formed in Rud's eyes as he told of her death at the birth of the Third Son, Mars. "Never say her name again," Rud told him. But seasons later, in a moment of drunken stupor, Rud had said, "You possess

Hela's quiet ways." At the words Eelin realized he carried part of Hela inside him which, strangely enough, made him feel closer to his father despite their differences. Hela kept their hearts as one.

Now as he hurried toward the Hall he covered his ears to drown out the celebratory sounds. He thought how hard it will be to tell this, his first lie, to Rud.

Eelin put the haunting thoughts aside. "I must be strong," he whispered. He toiled up the hill to the grotto and fingered the crystal in his pocket. Though the light had gone out, the crystal was warm, like a freshly-laid hen's egg. It trembled with energy whenever he touched it, giving him a feeling of power and at the same time calm. Touching it made him think of all things good, and the promise of more good to come. How can holding the key to the human world make me feel strong? he wondered. It will only bring trouble to me. Perhaps in the end it will bring peace for my people. He held fast to this thought and it gave him comfort.

The walls of the cavern had gradually widened, and as he neared the grotto the ceiling rose abruptly hundreds of foot-lengths into a dome. Lake Mered stood quiet, black as oil. Music from the Hall floated over the lake and was caught in the bowl. The Hall sounds swirled around him. He closed his eyes and opened them to see the torches at the lake. They circled Mered like a necklace of yellow quartz. Looming above the lake the shaft of the great Hall of Souls rose dazzlingly white, enclosed by toothy stalagmite fences that glowed an eerie green.

    The dirt road Eelin walked upon would soon become paved in the 120 marble steps that wound up to the massive door of the Hall.

    Along the right side of this road, tucked into the hills, were the meager shops, abandoned except for two forges, the wheel-maker, the bread maker, and the leathersman. The hills, and indeed the road itself, were once crowded with shops. But that was before the sickness. Over five-hundred trolls lost their lives to the human disease, and almost all of them lived in Haza.

    As Eelin climbed the steps to the Hall, he looked past the shops to what was left of the familial caves dug into the hills. Some of the abodes had richly carved stone entrances. Some were holes carved into the cavern wall. Many of the dwellings were connected by passageways that led to the rooms of cousins and grandparents. Most rooms were empty now.

The humans had brought such terrible disease, the legends said. But there were cures, the humans had claimed. "Let us return to our world for the medicines that will make you well," they said. Some trolls believed in the cures and wanted to try them, but Burg, Rud's father, had said no. Instead he killed the humans, killed them all before they found a way back. It was said some of the humans had escaped and were hiding in Iteria, but it was never proved.

What terrible trouble the humans had brought. And what good, Eelin thought. Wisdom. Animals for food, seeds, and the secrets of a world more advanced than ours.

Eelin looked back at the alcove where the passageway used to be. The opening to the human world was as though it had never existed. When the Way was open, it seemed as though the human world was merely an arm's length above Haza, as though he could dig with his bare hands and touch human soil. He knew in his heart this wasn't so. The human world and his world might as well be separated by ten thousand leagues of earth. He knew (others had tried) that he could dig for 100 lifetimes and never find sunlight. Because it wasn't there. Only the magic of the Saqa could make the two worlds come together.

    The Hall of Souls stood before him now. The white spire pierced the rust clouds that floated overhead thick as cloth. The pinnacle glittered like a beam of light, its tower tipped in silver. As Eelin climbed he saw behind the Hall the winding path that curved into the hill where perhaps 100 trolls lived. Besides the royal family, and the trolls scattered around distant pockets of Haza, this was all that was left of the kingdom, the clan.

    Pale reeds grew in the moist dirt next to the lake shore, where the water lapped against the rocks. A blind cat slept in the soft carbonweed nearby, and a young male troll played with a leather ball.

"Greetings, Waven," Eelin said.

The boy smiled. "Want to toss with me?"

"Perhaps later," Eelin said, mustering up a smile. He patted Waven's head as he passed by.

At last he reached the last of the marble steps, trudging up them with heavy legs. When he reached the grand door of the Hall he paused. The Hall, up close, looked as fragile as glass. Above the palace door burned seven lanterns, bubbling pale light onto the calcified, crusty stalagmite fence that grew to almost touch the sides of the palace. The light rippled over the stalagmites and made them seem alive, swaying to the music that came from behind the palace walls.

He patted his pocket that contained the crystal and a wave of power rolled through him. I must hide it, he thought. But not yet. I need its magic to get me through the meeting with Father.

Eelin pulled opened the massive silver doors and entered the marble courtyard. Low clouds hung in the airy room. Straight across the courtyard stood an archway where one could see through to the phosphorescent canyon. The canyon stretched for a long distance and was divided into squares that were many shades of green and brown. Tillers worked the soil and picked the food that grew by white phosphorescent light. The food was shared with the citizens of Haza, after the royal family were given the best of the harvest.

The noise of Mars's celebration had died down. Eelin crossed the courtyard. There were only 24 trolls living in the Hall of Souls, among them five cousins on Rud's side, Eelin's beloved Aunt Brule on his mother's side, advisors, servants, guards, and cooks. Rud's brother had long moved away after a bitter fight. It was said the fight was over humans, but Eelin never knew for sure.

Eelin turned down the corridor. A dozen scarified iron pillars lined both sides of the wide hallway. The ceiling had been finished in precious stones made into the shape of goats, prized for their milk. The first goats had been brought to Haza over a thousand seasons ago, gifts from the humans, along with special seeds that were sewn in the canyon to grow into feed. It was hard to look around Haza and not see the human influence. "But," he murmured, "the troll blade is unmatched in the human world."

As he walked down the corridor the yellow lanterns that lined the walls flung his shadow forward, and he saw how hunched and tired his form looked. He straightened himself.

Eelin came to the end of the hall and a pair of iron doors—the hall of banquets. The doors were richly carved and showed troll history; the birth of Suda, the first troll king, his great-great-grandfather Burg, enslaver of the Duots, the two-headed troll race.

Eelin patted his pocket, opened the creaking doors, and stepped inside.

Rud and Mars, the only trolls in the room, were seated together at the wooden table that stretched the entire length of the banquet room. The table was strewn with the remains of the feast, served in the best pewter bowls which were now toppled. A table lantern stood between Rud and Mars, and its harsh amber light made the dark circles under Rud's eyes seem cut to the bone.

"You are late, second son!" Rud called out in a drunken slur. Rud's words chilled the air.

He waved Eelin closer, then slapped a huge hand on the table.

Eelin shuddered. Blessed be the crystal for bringing me luck, he thought, upon seeing his father's drunken state. Mars smirked as he brought a chalice to his lips. He was, no doubt, clear-headed.

Eelin bowed slightly to both his father and brother as he approached the feast table. He stopped short, keeping a good distance. He sucked in his breath and said in a restrained voice, "Forgive my tardiness, Father. I have killed the human girl... but not without struggle." He pushed back a strand of hair that had stuck to his perspiration-slick temple as he watched Mars out of the corner of his eye.

And Mars watched him back. He stroked his cheek with the long nail of his forefinger. His nails were talon sharp and decorated with blue paint made from ground cobalt. He wore a finely cut shirt of moth silk, dyed from rare, darkest umber. Around his head was tied a new band of golden cloth, an obvious birthday present. Scattered on the table were other presents: a wooden carved statue of some rare bird (Eelin couldn't remember its name), a belt of precious rubies and obsidian, a sword of finest nicon. Another sword.

Rud smirked. "I would have killed it even as it squeezed through the Way." His face was bloated more than usual, and his eyes were the same blood red as the huge ruby he wore at his throat. He belched. "But, at least you have done it." The words seemed to fall out of his mouth onto the table.

"The Way is closed, Father," Eelin said. "But I did not get the teeth," he said sheepishly, looking down at his blood stained shirt. Better to tell his father before he was asked.

"Where are they? What did you do with them?" Rud gulped tuber wine and the brown liquid dribbled down his chin.

"I ate them, Father." Eelin avoided Rud's eyes, afraid his father could look into his mind and read his thoughts. "I did not think I would enjoy killing so." He reached into his pouch and pulled out the orange hair and waved it in the glow of the lanterns. It shimmered like a strand of fire. "I have a lock of the hair. Did you not hear the screams for mercy, my Lord?"

Rud snorted in anger. "I heard nothing! And do not ever disobey me again, or it will be your teeth I wear around my neck!" His voice rang like a deep bell in the great room.

Eelin continued to look down, but let his eyes wander upward to meet Rud's. "Forgive me," he said. "The human, the girl Annah, was so delicious. I became drunken in the excitement of my first kill." He paused. "And I must confess... I have something besides the hair." He withdrew the bloodied doll fingers from his pouch and laid them out in his palm. The blood had found its way to the porous roots of the fingers and had collected there, which gave the fingers a realistic appearance. "I have the girl's fingers." He wet his lips. "I did not know how tasty the human would be. This is all that remains of it."

Rud shrugged. "I've tasted better. Did you drink the blood from the neck?"

"I did, Father, I did." Eelin's hand went to his shirt. He hoped his father's eyes were sharp enough to see the blood spatters. His ears burned. Can Father tell how frightened I am? he wondered. Can he tell I am lying? Or is he too wine-soaked?

Eelin cupped the fingers carefully in his hand, to keep them in shadow. They are so small, he thought. So white. He plucked one of the fingers and raised it to his mouth. "In the name of Rud," he said reverently, and dropped it on his tongue and began to chew as quickly as he could. He took the other finger and raised it to his mouth.

"Wait!" Mars said, looking at Eelin with cold yellow eyes. "I would like one of the human fingers." He gave Rud a pleading glance, and a smile flickered across his lips. "From the human, this—*Annah*."

Eelin forced his eyes to stare at Rud and tried to still his racing heart. He wiped all emotion from his face. He knew if he looked at Mars for even an instant the contempt would explode from him.

Rud squeezed Mars's arm. "Be still, Youngest. It is Eelin's honor to eat all of his first kill." Rud nodded at Eelin as a way of saying, "Continue."

Eelin dropped the finger into his mouth and chewed it and swallowed it, and afterward smiled in satisfaction. "Finished," he said.

Rud bowed, and closed his eyes slowly in a relieved way. "Finished."

Mars leaned back in his leather chair. He tapped his long fingernails on the table, watching Eelin with narrowed eyes, staring into him, tapping, tapping.

Eelin felt his eyes glaring back at Mars. He knows, Eelin thought. He *knows*.

· FOUR ·

When Eelin was small, he took delight in caring for his younger brother. He did it for himself, because Mars would have no part of him, or anyone else, watching over him. Even back then Eelin knew his brother would never care about another troll, not even clan. But rather than think his brother odd or evil, Eelin thought himself weak. "Trolls are strong. We do not worry ourselves with feelings and care— we do not show emotion," he told himself. And <u>he</u> felt odd for having to always check himself when the caring feelings arose. As a small troll he did not know how to prepare himself for the Age of Wisdom other than to quell those feelings and try to replace them with not caring about others. It was to be the most difficult task of his life.

Now, in the hall of banquets, Eelin looked at the gifts arranged on the table in front of Mars. "I too have a present for you, Brother," he said kindly.

"Well, go fetch it, Heir!" Rud cried, clapping his fat brown hands together. "And join us for what is left of the celebration." He was jolly, anxious to celebrate, but Eelin knew that before he returned with the gift for Mars, Rud would be passed out on the table.

"Yes, Father." Eelin bowed deeper than usual and turned to leave the room.

He had a sudden thought that made him feel giddy. What would Mars and Rud say if they knew I had the stone in my possession? I do not like having it with my body. I fear Rud can feel the magic with his keen sense. He knows more about the Saqa stone than he lets on, I am sure of that. Perhaps he knows as much as the Chronicler herself.

Eelin patted his pocket as he trudged down the hall and up the circular stairway to his chamber. He opened the door with the key he wore at his ankle, and pressed the door open. The familiar tall windows and furnishings of onyx and rare woods greeted him and he felt tremendous relief as he closed and locked the door. He went to the window and looked out over Lake Mered.

"What am I going to do with Annah?" he asked, leaning forward to let the tangy, moist air fill his lungs. "Until I make a new Way..." The answer to this question was obvious. "Iteria. It must be. Annah will be safe with Princess Mave. Father would never risk war with Iteria over one human. I pray."

He went to his wooden clothes chest and opened the lid decorated with royal iron arrowheads. Lying on top of his clothes was the present for Mars that he had commissioned by the smith at the Royal Forge. It was a quill pen of heavy nicon, inlaid with diamonds in the shape of a sunburst, and wrapped in precious goat hide. Eelin knew his brother could not write, moreover, the allusion to the human sun was beyond insulting. This was a cruel present.

"Perhaps," he muttered, "Mars could draw circles on paper with the blood of the small animals he likes to kill for sport."

In the same wooden chest, underneath his clothes, were two books. They were as precious as anything Eelin owned, though he knew he could never appreciate them the way they were meant to be appreciated. He could not read, he could only look at the letters, touch them, and feel the fine paper. He could only imagine what stories the books contained.

It was said his mother Hela could read. Only a few words, but she had trusted a human to teach her. She had learned, it was said, just before her death.

Eelin brought out the books from the chest and lay them on top of the clothes. The books had fallen though the passageway before Annah was taken.

"Perhaps she can teach me," he whispered.

Eelin prepared to change his blood stained shirt in honor of the celebration, but then thought better of it. Wearing the bloody shirt would remind his brother and father—and himself that he was now and forever heir to the Chair of Light, and soon to be King of Haza.

He reached into his trouser pocket, withdrew the Saqa crystal and buried it in the bottom corner of the chest underneath his clothes.

And now I must get back to the celebration, he thought as he took the gift for Mars and closed the heavy wooden lid. He locked the clothes chest. As he moved to leave he thought: I will tell Father that it is time to make the journey to Iteria. I will ask his blessing, and he will give it, now that I have proven myself. Soon it will be time to talk of two clans as one under my rule.

He stopped at the window and stared vacantly at the black lake. "Father will give his blessing all right," he said with a smirk. "Now that I have killed the human."

Rud was nearly unconscious when Eelin returned to the celebration hall.

A black cat stretched itself out on the banquet table. Mars stroked the blessed animal with one hand while staring stonily into his goblet. He had removed the golden band from his head and it lay folded on the table in front of him. Neat little folds, perfect folds.

"A birthday wish, Brother," Eelin said, setting the gift in front of Mars.

Mars unwrapped the pen. "A gift more fitting for yourself," he muttered, jabbing the pen point into the wooden table. "You are more human than troll," he said coldly, without looking up. The remark was considered highly insulting to Hazans.

Eelin smiled vaguely and said under his breath, "If any troll is clever enough to learn to write it would be you, dear Brother." Mars hated humans with a burning passion. Eelin said in a louder voice, "May you have many seasons of good health."

Mars seemed taken aback by Eelin's gentle words. He stopped jabbing at the table and set the pen down.

"Mother had a pen like this I am told," Eelin continued in an offhand way. "I cannot help but think of her as you celebrate the day of your birth."

Mars's face reddened.

"I am sorry you could not know her, Brother," Eelin said. He circled the banquet table and put his hand on his father's shoulder. Rud's head bobbed slowly, and his eyelids flickered. Into Rud's ear he whispered, "I make ready to journey to Iteria and will return soon, Father."

Rud nodded and said something unintelligible, and Eelin gently laid his father's head down on the table. "Sleep well, my Lord," he said. He turned and swept out of the room without so much as a glance at his brother.

Eelin did not go straight to his chamber. Instead, he walked down the corridor and crossed the marble courtyard to the west wing. There he climbed a set of silver-inlaid stairs that led to the pinnacle of the Hall of Souls. At the top of the stairs stood a marble door edged in bloodstones. He pressed his shoulder to the heavy door and it swung silently inward.

The white marble room with its domed ceiling of gold leaf was the smallest room in the Hall, but it was the grandest, and the most important. This, the throne room, contained the Chair of Light, where kings sat to make important decisions and receive advice from the advisors, the Second Lords.

Eelin crossed over to the gleaming Chair that stood in the very center of the round room. The Chair was hand forged of nicon with huge diamonds pressed into the backrest. The feet of the chair were clawed like a cat's, and into each claw was pressed a green emerald.

Eelin sat down. Carved into the chair's gleaming nicon arms were the profiled faces of past kings, and Eelin knew his face would soon be among those images. A place for him had been reserved on the left-hand arm, just below Rud's. Iron had been poured into the carvings to make them show up against the silvery background. His face would be forever etched, forever remembered in troll history.

Eelin ran his hands over the smooth metal. He smiled in anticipation of the Hazans and the Iterians united as one kingdom. And now I have the crystal as well, he thought. It has come full circle. I am as my father was when he first sat here. I am the keeper of the last stone. But unlike my father, I will use the stone for good. The Way will open once again. When I am king, trolls and humans will once again trade wisdom. His heart was full; his breath came fast in anticipation.

And what of the human diseases? Can I trust the humans and their cures? he asked himself. Tye legend said human medicines were made of plants and animals more deadly than the plagues themselves. At least with magic, in the hands of a wise one, you knew the outcome. Perhaps the medicines could live beside magic, Eelin thought. All the more reason to unite the kingdoms and gather the Iterian's vast knowledge of sorcery. Eelin shook his head, sorry that he knew neither medicines nor magic.

Will the Iterians and Hazans live well together? he wondered. The Iterians are simple, though strong-willed. Mave is the key to the union. If only she would grow up and accept her destiny. Grow up. I will change into human before that happens!

Eelin had not realized that his eyes were closed. He opened them slowly to see Mars standing in the doorway, watching him, sneering. How long Mars had been there, Eelin did not know. But now Mars was gone with a flutter of silk and the glint of a new sword.

※

Eelin took his best nicon sword from above his bed and wrapped it, in its scabbard, in a feather-woven blanket which would serve as a bedroll. He gathered clothes for the journey: a plain white shirt, leather breeches, a hooded cloak for Annah. He did not wear his princely robe of rabbit and iron arrowheads. Instead he wore rough-hewn trousers and a dark leather shirt and black cloth cloak that reached past his knees. He placed the crystal in the pocket of his trousers once again, this time wrapped in a square of moth silk. He checked the small yellow pouch at his belt that contained the lock of Annah's hair and the Saqa seed.

"It would be foolish to leave the seed in my chamber," he said. At the words, a feeling of sadness overcame him. "I will never see Haza again," he whispered. "Now that Mars knows." As a precaution, he placed the stone and seed in separate pockets.

Into a leather travel bag he placed the two books from his clothes chest. There were colorful drawings on the book covers. He couldn't wait to give them back to Annah. He smiled at the thought of pleasing her with gifts from her world.

He took his bag and bedroll down to the kitchen and set them on the table. He opened a tall cupboard, found a round pouch into which he packed food for the four league journey to Iteria. When he was finished he brought his things around to the stable. There in the stable he took down the largest leather saddlebag which hung on great iron hooks on the stone walls. He harnessed his favorite mule, Salt, and laid the saddlebag over her back. Salt was a young, strong albino who was calm of nerve. He took the sword wrapped in the blanket and placed it under Salt's girth strap. Of course the thick blanket was for Annah. So were the candles he tucked into one of the saddlebags.

Into the saddlebags he also placed a pouch of dried, salted meat strips, felton fish, dried goat cheese, and soft bread he had taken from the kitchen's huge storage jars.

He collected good water in a bladder which he tied to the saddlebag. He packed dried seeds and vega root for the mule. He patted his large belt pouch which held the sharpening stone for the belt knife which never left his side. The flint for the candles had gone into the little pouch that held the seed and Annah's hair.

He stole away without sound, not difficult because most of Haza was asleep now. It was nearing the new rotation. He led Salt carefully around the lake, her hooves silent as they sunk into the damp ground. He sensed the vague shadows deep in the pool, burial grounds for those not of royal blood, including humans, and of course the trolls tainted by human disease. Were the bones of humans scattered along the water's bottom like the bones of chickfowl on a platter? He tried not to think about that.

He reached the spot where the passageway had been, where Annah had come to Haza. "Salt," he whispered, drawing the mule toward the silent alcove. He patted the top of her head and gave her a mouthful of seeds. He looked up into the spot where the hole had been, where the blue sheet had floated and the scarlet Saqa had grown. The passageway was completely closed, of course, and already the water had begun its drip, drip, engorging the heavy earth.

It was as though the Way had never been.

The two worlds were, at this spot, forever sealed off from each other. No amount of digging could reopen the Way. This was magic. A hundred and thirty seasons Eelin had lived and still he could not make sense of it. A long time ago he had convinced himself that there was no reason to understand, that he needed only to believe. Magic was best left for wizards anyway. But this much he knew: The magic of the Saqa was ancient, and had evolved, like the trolls, since life began.

Eelin bent down and saw, to his horror, that all remnants of the flower were gone. "Mars," he muttered. A shiver went though him, pricking up the hair on the back of his neck. He patted the crystal in his pocket and was instantly calmed. Now he made haste toward the meadow, pulling the mule along as quickly as she would go.

As he neared Far Light meadow he began to worry about Annah. Would she still be there?

What if she had run? What if Mars had reached her?

He walked close to the mule, stroking her neck, looking at the bag that held the books for Annah. She will read to me if there is time, he thought. And it will remind me of my mother Hela.

When he reached Far Light, he half expected to see Annah curled up, sobbing. Instead he found her bent over a shallow pool, stirring the milky water with a staff of green stalagmite. From a distance away Eelin thought he caught the glitter of her ocean-colored eyes.

"You are still here," Eelin said when he reached her. He was unable to contain his pleasure. He grinned.

"Where else could I go?" Annah said softly. On the ground beside her lay her book and doll.

Eelin bent down next to her and gazed at his reflection in the pool, at their faces touching. "It is done," he said without emotion.

She made ribbons in the water, making their reflections wiggle. "Done," she repeated.

I wonder if she finds me ugly, Eelin thought. He sensed that much of the fear had left her, but this did not mean she found him acceptable.

She stood and patted Salt's head. "And so," she said. "Did your father really believe you? Did he believe you'd killed me?"

Eelin rose. "I pray that he did, though I cannot be certain..."

"Then I can go home now."

Eelin stiffened. "First, you must eat." He reached for the packs. "Surely you must be hungry."

"And then you will take me home?"

Eelin took a deep breath. "Sending you home is more complicated than you think."

"But you said after you convinced your father..."

"It is my brother Mars that I am worried about."

"I see."

"He will come for us—for you, no doubt. There will not be time to send you home as long as he is—" He finished, under his breath, "Alive."

"Your brother, he thinks like your father? He hates humans, I mean."

"He fancies himself the next king," Eelin said. Instinctively his hand went to his jeweled necklace.

Annah stared at his hands fingering the huge stones. Her mouth opened, but no words came out for a long moment. "You're a Prince."

"I am," Eelin said. "Heir to the Chair of Light."

"I knew you were no ordinary troll."

Eelin felt her eyes looking at him in a new way which made him uncomfortable. "We are not safe here," he said quickly. "In fact, we must journey to a distant kingdom." He reached into the saddle bag and drew out the gray woolen cloak and handed it to Annah. "You must wear this for your safety. If a stranger approaches, wrap your body and cover your face." He pulled close his own black cloak.

She donned the cloak. "So when you are king you will send me home?" She looked into his eyes without concealing her expression of hope.

"When I am king, yes..." he said, praying she would not question him further about going home. He knew it could be many seasons before he became king. Rud could live a long while. And he knew it would take many rotations to learn the crystal's magic and learn how to grow the Saqa and begin the Way. "The animal can support your weight if you wish to ride," he said, abruptly changing the subject. "And there is food. Eat."

"I can walk," Annah said. She stroked the mule's bristly white fur. "What is his name?"

"Her name is Salt," Eelin said. "I'm sure she won't mind carrying your book and doll. That is if you can part with them. They're sure to get heavy by journey's end."

Annah obliged, placing them in the leather pack Eelin held open for her.

"Now have some good water," Eelin urged. "And a bit of dried meat." He brought out the small water bag and a long leather pouch. Inside the pouch were several strips of dried chickfowl. There were also chunks of dried felton, the best silvery fish taken from the lake of good water. He took a piece of felton and handed it to Annah and held the small water bladder until she was ready to drink.

"I guess I was hungry," she said, when she had finished eating and drinking.

Eelin brought out the books and handed them to Annah. "These are for you," he said gruffly.

Annah held them to her and smiled. She seemed happy, but there were tears in her eyes. "Thank you," she said.

"I expect you to read them to me," Eelin told her. He took the books and tucked them back into the bag. "But now it is time to go east. To Iteria, and Princess Mave's kingdom. Do not worry. It is safe there. No disease. No humans have walked there…"

"What do you mean?"

"No passageways. They have not seen humans."

"It must be far away," Annah said.

"Far yet close," Eelin replied.

He began to walk slowly, leading the mule by its strap. He prayed to the gods for safe journey to Iteria. "If the gods see fit to honor my plea," he promised himself, "I will ask nothing more of them."

· FIVE ·

Annah was glad she could see in this meadow of glowing stalagmites called Far Light. Eelin had warned her that the road they walked upon would turn to low tunnel once again, that there would be no lanterns or torches to light the way. The air would not stay cool, but would become hot, full of ash. But now, above their heads, cool water dripped steadily, soaking the calcified sprouts in the ground.

"I hope it will not be too dark," Annah said. She did not like dark. In the dark he might change his mind. He could kill her in the dark. He could kill her in the light, too, for that matter.

"A troll would never complain about lack of light," Eelin said, laughing. "Imagine! A human in my world." He touched her hand lightly and said in a gentle tone, "In time your eyes will learn to see in this darkness."

In time. This meant she would be all right. Annah found it hard to believe, the idea of seeing in the dark. It was impossible. After a while she realized that what she was really feeling was the fear that she would never see the light of her world again. "I may as well be wearing a sack over my head," she muttered. "At any rate," she went on, "just because other humans were able to see doesn't mean I will. You can't know for sure. You said yourself I'm the first human you have known."

"The Chronicler said it was so," Eelin replied.

"And what is a Chronicler?" she asked, peering into his enormous eyes. The eyes were not darkest brown as she had first thought; flecks of gold were there too. If you look at just the eyes, she thought, he looks human.

"The Chronicler is one who knows the human world," Eelin said. "In Haza City such a troll would be stoned if she did not lurk in secret, and that is why I have not seen her with my own eyes. But others have seen her."

"You wouldn't stone her?" Annah asked.

Eelin shook his head no, tossing his long braids side to side.

"Why are you so different from the others in your kingdom?" Annah asked. "Why do you like humans so much, when your father and brother hate them?"

He shrugged. "I can't say that I like them all, because you are the only one I have known. But perhaps I take after my mother Hela, who did not share my father's hatred of humankind. There are others like me in Haza. But they keep quiet. They must."

"You risk your life by having me around," she said.

"I risk much more than that," he said.

She tried to understand. A prince has many people to worry about, she supposed. "And I'll be safe in Iteria with Princess Mave?" she asked.

"Safe enough." He chuckled.

"And where will you go, Eelin?"

He didn't answer.

"Mave," Annah repeated. It sounded like a human name. "Is she like you?"

Eelin smiled. "Troll-ish like me? Wild, frightening?"

"I mean, is she young like you? You are young?"

He shrugged. "I have seen much for my time."

Annah studied him as he spoke, and thought they were the same age, but the longer she looked, the older he seemed. There was a weariness about him, a seriousness, or perhaps it was merely the wisdom that went with being a prince. Without wisdom, how could he rule?

"My father would have my teeth if he found out I disobeyed him," Eelin continued.

"He would kill his own son?"

"Of course."

Annah shuddered. How strange and barbaric trolls are. How unlike humans. She had never believed that trolls were real, but once when she was younger she had told herself that if they *were* real, and if she ever encountered one she would feel superior because, according to the stories, they were no more intelligent than dogs. But now, with Eelin, she did not feel superior. She felt curiosity, mostly. Because he was so different from her.

"Do you think you will ever get to be king?" she asked.

He looked straight ahead and continued walking.

"I'm never going home, am I?" she asked after a while. She looked around for a door, a way out.

Eelin stopped and turned to face her. He reached into his trouser pocket. "This," he said in an exasperated voice, "this is the way home," and he pressed a pale blue crystal into her palm.

"The light in the flower!" Annah said, closing her hand around the crystal. The jewel was smooth and warm as though it had sat in the sun all day. She opened her hand. "You took this from the flower?" she asked, unable to take her eyes away from the magnificent stone. It was magic, she knew it—she felt its electricity dancing up the muscles of her arm.

"I took it on the way to my Father's," Eelin said. "I had to take it, so he would believe you were dead. You see, when the human dies, the flower dies, the stone dies. Everything dies."

"But I'm not dead, and so—?" she asked, bringing the crystal to her eyes, looking though it into Eelin's eyes that looked like round caramels.

"The magic is untouched," he said matter-of-factly.

"Well then the crystal can make a new passageway." She squinted at the stone, hoping to find a streak of light, of life.

"But first a new flower must be grown from seed, and then the stone must be placed inside the flower," Eelin went on. "I suppose there is some magic needed to make it grow, and I'm afraid I don't know more than that. Rud knows. And of course the Chronicler. When I take the Chair, I will know that and more..."

"I have grown many flowers at the school," Annah volunteered.

He smiled. "Do not worry," he said, taking the stone from her and putting it back into his pocket. "We will find the Way again."

"I certainly hope so," Annah said in a cynical voice. She felt instantly sorry for that and hoped Eelin did not pick up on her tone. She was tired. She yawned, covering her mouth with her hand. She had been fighting sleep for a long while. Now, after seeing the stone, and knowing its magic held the way home, and feeling more certain that Eelin wouldn't harm her, she had given herself permission to relax. "Do you think we could rest for a while?" she asked. She reached out her hand and brushed it against a luminous boulder. They had come to the end of the stalagmite plain, she knew, for ahead was a pair of round tunnels staring at her like huge black eyes.

"Yes," Eelin said. "You should sleep, if only for a short while."

She lowered herself to the ground and leaned back against the rock. "I am so tired."

Eelin sat down next to her and before she realized it she was using his shoulder as a pillow. "What time is it?" she asked him groggily.

"Time for sleep," he said in a soothing voice, and she could not help but oblige.

☼☼

The play room at Seton House was noisy. Annah sat in the center of the circle with Abbi tucked into her lap and a book in her hand. Around her sat the children, the younger ones in front, some with thumbs in their mouths. Behind her, against the wall, was the wooden toy box, overflowing with toys, most of which had been donated by the Church of the Honorable. How kind the Church has been this month, she thought.

"Today," she said loudly, so the children would quiet down, "I will read the story of Brave Mouse." A smile grew on the children's faces as it always did at story time.

The children settled and she opened the small book with the cloth cover. She began to read. "Miggon Mouse scurried through the cupboards in search of food. He was worried about his wife, Minerva, who was feeling a bit under the weather..."

The door to the play room opened softly and Headmistress Downing poked her head inside.

Annah glanced up and nodded politely. Miss Downing summoned Annah with a frenzied wave of the hand. She mouthed something which Annah could not understand.

"Gisella, will you continue the story please?" Annah asked the lanky twelve-year-old girl in the back row. Gisella rose. "Thank you." The girl took Annah's place on the chair and Annah followed Miss Downing down the hall toward the office.

"I have a surprise for you," Miss Downing said without looking back as she hurried down the hall. Her black lace-up shoes clunked noisily on the wooden floor. Her gray hair was wrapped at her neck in a neat braid, and the braid had three shades of gray woven into it, Annah noticed for the first time.

Miss Downing went into her office, swept up to her desk and stood behind it, fingers playing the wooden surface like a piano. Seated in a chair facing the desk was an attractive middle-aged woman. The woman turned around in her chair and smiled at Annah when she entered the room. Annah noticed the woman's eyes were glassy, as though she had been crying, or as though she had a head cold.

Miss Downing waved Annah to the chair next to the woman and said, "Annah, I'd like you to meet Mrs. Atherton. Mrs. Atherton, here is Annah."

Annah and Mrs. Atherton shook hands, Annah with a bend at the knees. Annah took her seat and clasped her hands in her lap. Out of the corner of her eye she looked at Mrs. Atherton. Her eyes were pale blue violet. Her flowing dress had cobalt blue birds embroidered along the hem, and from her waist hung a gold cord with a bell at the end of it that tinkled when she shifted her weight in the wooden chair. She is like a bird, Annah thought. Light, and airy, ready to fly away. Annah tried not to stare at the woman, who seemed to be trying not to stare at her. The woman is pleasant, Annah thought. And her dark red hair is long and flowing, not confined. She is probably an artist or maybe even a singer, Annah thought.

"Annah," Miss Downing said, "I have wonderful news." She peered over her glasses at Mrs. Atherton.

Annah felt her eyes widen. Am I being adopted? she wondered. All at once she was filled with feelings of both happiness and dread. She had lived at Seton House all her life. It was home. But not her permanent home.

"As you know," Miss Downing continued, "every so often a child from Seton is given the wonderful opportunity for adoption." She looked into Annah's eyes.

Annah bit her lip to stop it from quivering. She took deep breaths to keep her heart from beating so hard.

"Of course, there is always much cause for celebration when this happens, and at the same time there is a sadness when we have to say good-bye."

Mrs. Atherton dabbed her eyes with a handkerchief. On her lap sat a black crocheted purse, open, with a folded paper peeking out.

"Yes, it is indeed a bittersweet moment when a child is adopted," Miss Downing went on.

Annah felt her head nod slowly as her fingers curled around the chair to keep her from falling over.

"But," Miss Downing said in a cautious tone, "but this is not the case with you, Annah."

A lump grew in Annah's throat. She stared at Miss Downing. Her nose caught a whiff of Mrs. Atherton, who smelled of wild anise and finger-paint. The combination of smells was vaguely familiar and Annah wondered if she had dreamed them once.

Miss Downing cleared her throat. "Annah," she announced, "I'd like you to meet your mother."

Annah stopped breathing. Every muscle in her body seized up. Her chair seemed to float off the floor, then it seemed to spin.

Mrs. Atherton said softly, turning her face to Annah, "Yes, Annah, I am your mother."

The words fluttered into Annah's ears. She mouthed the word mother. She was unable to speak it aloud.

ಬಾಬ

    Annah batted moisture from her nose and slowly opened her eyes. She was lying on her back, and a cool gray cloud billowed around her like a scarf, blurring her vision. What a strange dream this is, she thought. She felt relaxed and pleasantly buoyant.

    A pair of shadowy eyes came into view and studied her, but she didn't mind, because with the eyes came breath that warmed her. As she stared at the huge eyes, a face came into hazy focus, and she was sure it was a kind face. The face began to fade, and Annah reached out to touch it, to get it back. She stroked the face blindly, and it was full of soft, short hairs. She withdrew her hand as the mouth wrinkled into a smile.

    The image sharpened as the knowledge of where she was and who the face belonged to came rushing into her thoughts.

    Eelin bent over her smiling.

    Annah let out a small cry just as Eelin put his arm around her shoulder and helped her sit up.

"How long have I been asleep?" Annah asked. Now she was wide awake, blinking through steamy clouds. Around her had been placed a feather blanket, and under her head had been placed a pillow of silken material.

"Not long," Eelin said. "Barely one rotation."

Annah said, "I had the strangest dream."

"Did you?"

"I dreamed I had a mother." She put her fingers to her temples.

"You don't have one?"

"I was told she died when I was born. I tried not to believe it. And now, I don't know. The dream was so real. Not like a dream at all, but a sort of prophesy. Do you understand?"

Eelin cocked his head and nodded. His brows slanted downward which gave him a sort of sad, inquisitive expression. "I have had many dreams like that," he said gently. "I awoke, sweat-soaked, certain that what I dreamed had really taken place. But often they were not pleasant dreams like yours. They were frightening."

"Mine should have been pleasant," Annah said thoughtfully. "But it was scary. I dreamed I met my mother for the first time and had to leave the orphanage." She added hastily, "An orphanage is for children who have no parents."

"This dream does not sound scary," Eelin said.

"She was a total stranger."

"Except that she was part of you," Eelin said. "I do not remember my mother very well. Just one or two events, that is all."

"No?"

"She died at the birth of the youngest son. My brother Mars."

"My mother is probably dead, too," Annah said, trying to make him feel better. "It was, after all, only a dream. And dreams don't come true."

Eelin said, "Truth has many faces." He stood abruptly and went to the mule. He turned and said, "And what is truth?"

Annah nodded. "It changes, doesn't it? Just a few hours ago I was sure that you were going to kill me."

Eelin looked away. Moving his hands over the mule's pack, he took down a small bag and handed it to Annah. "Good water," he said in a voice full of respect.

The bag was warm, made of bristly fur, but the water inside was cold, and slippery as though laced with oil. It tasted sweet.

"If you are hungry we can eat," Eelin offered.

Annah rose. "No, I'm fine."

Eelin gathered up the silken pillow, which Annah saw was a shirt. He rolled the blanket around an iron scabbard that was strapped to the mule. Without speaking he picked up the leather lead tied to Salt's neck and began to walk. Annah followed.

"The good part about having a mother," she said, "is feeling like you belong to someone who thinks like you do and cares about you."

Eelin looked back and nodded.

"At least, that's what I imagine."

"Then it is Truth."

Soon the light began to fade just like night gathering, Annah thought. The cavern walls changed from pale green to darkest brown. The air grew warm and hung heavy like a summer night. The smoke reddened. After a short while Annah could no longer see the smoke, but could smell it stronger, and as the sounds around her became more distinct she realized it had grown dark as midnight. To her ears came the clump, clump of Salt's hooves, and the soft pad of Eelin's bare feet on the damp ground. A distant hammer struck metal. Stumbling through the blackness, she clung to Eelin's elbow and picked her way over pebbles and tripped over what felt like mounds of straw.

"What is that sound, and what are they burning?" she asked.

"The sound comes from the forges—hammers on steel and iron, and nicon for swords. The metal burning is what you smell. Surely your legends tell of trolls and their fine metalwork."

"Yes. And stone cutting. The legends say that trolls have more than one head. That they eat humans, and that they have ten times more gold than the gold in my world."

"You may be right about the gold," Eelin said, smiling.

Thus they continued on their journey for what seemed to Annah like half a day.

And then Eelin said, "We should sleep now. You are used to sleeping in darkness?"

Annah answered, "I'm used to sleeping in the dark, yes. But I don't know if it's day or night."

"Your body will find its own time," Eelin said.

"My body tells me I'm hungry and tired," Annah said.

They ate a small meal of bread and crumbly cheese, and soon thereafter they lay down next to each other, Annah on the feather blanket, Eelin on a plot of humid earth.

Annah closed her eyes and listened to the delicate sounds of Eelin breathing next to her, and to the distant hammering of metal. "However will I sleep? There's no moon, no stars..." was the last thing she remembered saying.

· SIX ·

They awoke and continued on their journey. Eelin smiled, glad that, for Annah's sake, the dark gave way to pale light, although with it came the fire, which he was sure would burn Annah's lungs. And there was the heat. It was the heat he didn't like; he had never grown used to it. Next to him Annah grimaced and coughed while the chink of hammers shattered the silence.

"Where are we now?" Annah asked, cupping her hands over her face.

"Geyser Plain just there," he answered, peering out at the smoky flatland. The plain was once well populated. Sad, that, he thought. As he looked around, he watched for bandits known to roam this open territory. He dared not mention it to Annah for fear of frightening her. The stone in his pocket gave him some comfort, though he knew he could not count on it to save their lives. Only the sword on Salt's back could do that. The ruby hilt faced him, tucked into its scabbard wrapped in the blanket. He could have the blade in one breath.

He led Salt to the only safe spot on the plain, a semicircle of boulders. He rubbed her neck. She buried her nose in his chest and he said, "You are a lucky creature. There are no worries for you, are there?"

Eelin and Annah ate a small meal of water and dried meat. Soon they would cross into the region of Barden, which was even more dangerous than this spot for bandits, but after Barden would come the border of Iteria, and the safety of its matted forests.

Annah sat next to Eelin, drinking water with eyes tightly closed. Tears came to her eyes.

"You will soon get used to the smell," Eelin said. "They burn many kinds of metals at the forge and you will know by the smell which ones are burning." He nodded at a high hill in the distance where fires exploded into red clouds.

"I have a lot to get used to," Annah said, blinking. "How long have I been here?"

He answered thoughtfully, "You have been here six rotations."

"Six rotations?"

"The geysers. That is how we measure time," he said. "The geysers erupt reliably."

She translated the time, based on what she supposed must be accurate. "Twelve hours," she said. "I didn't hear anything."

"It is a rumbling felt underfoot, a touch that must be understood. And now it is time to go," he said urgently. He stood up and cocked his head to listen. "Time to go."

He gazed at the hills, and at higher hills beyond. Barden. The road threaded upward, and was dotted with glowing green stones that marked the path. There was a river, too, like a dark snake that followed the path and never crossed it.

"It's hard to believe we're underground," Annah said. She walked beside Eelin now, holding a square of bread in her hand that she nibbled on leisurely. "The ceiling of the cave is so high I can't see where it ends. There are clouds like the ones back home. The only thing missing is the blue."

Eelin peered up at the mist. "I can't even imagine what that is like," he said. "To see blue above all this. The Chronicler says that in the human world, rain pours down from the clouds and the air is made fresh. The sun brings a rainbow of many colors stretched across the sky." He looked at Annah inquisitively. "A rain-bow..." He thought of the iron bow he used to snare beasts and smiled at the way a word could mean many things.

"The Chronicler is right," Annah said wistfully. "It's beautiful back home."

Eelin noticed the sad tone to Annah's voice. I would miss my home if there were rainbows, he thought. She will see her home again, I promise her that. And then an odd thought surfaced: I do want her to go home, don't I? She has not become like a pet, has she? "We have many colors here," he said. But he knew his colors could never compete with a rainbow. He knew he could not keep her here.

They crossed the desolate plain in two rotations and reached the temple. "Tenon," Eelin said reverently as the quartz columns, encrusted with white stalagmites, came into view. The clouds moved across the temple, shrouding it and making it look as through it were a cloud itself.

"What is Tenon?" Annah asked.

"The Temple of Tenon," Eelin said. "I have not been to this place in many seasons. I do not remember it being so decayed." He led the mule closer and Annah followed, until they reached the steep temple stairs.

Eelin watched as Annah stood in front of the stairs for a long moment. "How strange, unearthly, beautiful," she said. "It looks like it's made of ice. It reminds me of the ancient Greek temple I learned about in school," she said. "The Parthenon..."

Eelin said, "I hope Tenon looks like your Parthenon." He patted Salt's head and fed her from the seed bag.

"It looks enchanted," Annah murmured, edging toward the steps. "When was the temple built?"

"In the 14th Age, by trolls who had learned from a human builder of temples. When humankind walked in Haza. Tenon was once a place of worship..."

"I must go inside," Annah said, turning.

Eelin winced. He stepped in front of her and waved her away from the steps. "You mustn't. You should never enter a crumbling..."

"Oh, please," Annah said, circling him.

"It isn't safe," Eelin said. "There may be..."

But she scrambled up the steep steps anyway and looked down at him from the top. "It's lovely," she said, spinning in a small circle. She ran farther inside until Eelin could no longer see her.

Eelin groaned as he tied Salt's lead to a small boulder. He ran up the steps and followed Annah into the temple. The quartz walls were eerily white, and made him shiver as though cold wind grew inside him. He did not feel the god's protective presence the way he always did when he came here, and this made him uneasy.

He watched Annah as she tiptoed toward the back of the pillared room and stared up at the marble sculptures that edged the ceiling.

Eelin stepped over a wide crack in the floor where the ground had opened. "The gods have cursed this place," he muttered. "That is why I cannot sense them here."

"Where does this hallway lead?" Annah asked. She disappeared into a dark passageway before Eelin could stop her.

"We must go now!" Eelin whispered firmly. He sensed he should not shout.

A moment later there came a shriek. Eelin's hand went to his belt knife and he raced toward the passageway, muttering curses.

He was met by five trolls pushing Annah toward him. One held a nicon saber to her back.

"Let her go!" Eelin said, unable to take his eyes from the saber. It was a fine blade for such ragged trolls. "She means you no harm. We are just passing through." He clutched his cloak to him as he attempted to shroud his face.

The largest of the trolls had a purple scar across his nose. With the knife tip, he loosened the tie on Annah's cloak, and it fell crumpled at her feet. "It is true!" he growled. The other four trolls stepped back.

"A human in Haza!" the troll continued. "I have seen one like this many seasons ago." He turned to the others. "Do not touch it! It is diseased." His foul breath came out in sharp gusts. Eelin could smell it from where he stood.

"What would Rud say if he knew you were hiding a human?" the troll said, poking Annah with the blade and glaring at Eelin.

Annah's face went white as the marble walls.

Eelin cleared his throat. "Rud knows about the human. He has ordered me to kill it; even now we go to the altar." He lowered the cloak from his head. "I am Prince Eelin and I command you to release her." Eelin fingered the necklace at his neck. "I am Second Son of Rud and heir to the..."

"And I'm Rud himself," the leader interrupted. The other trolls snorted and laughed.

The smallest troll, a wiry one with long fingers, demanded, "We'll have your weapons and that pretty necklace you're wearing."

Eelin's neck stiffened and his eyes burned hatred. He was outraged that these soulless beings would have his necklace. But he knew what he must do. "They are yours," he said, keeping all emotion from his tone. "If you release the human."

The leader spoke, after some thought, "It seems an even trade."

Eelin tossed his knife to the floor and unclasped his necklace and handed it to the troll. "There, now let the human go."

"Empty your pouches!" the leader said.

Eelin opened his large pouch and removed the sharpening stone and threw it to the ground. He untied his side pouch full of silver coin and tossed it down as well. He opened the yellow pouch that held the seed, flint, and lock of Annah's hair. "See, this one is empty of coin," he said, holding it open without revealing the small things inside. "Now give her to me."

The leader picked up the things from the ground. He poked Eelin's trouser pocket with the tip of his knife blade. "What's that in your pocket?"

Eelin watched Annah close her eyes and mouth a silent word. Not the stone! His heart jammed up against his ribs. "It's just a rock I found," he said," his voice faltering.

"Give it up," the troll demanded.

"The girl first," Eelin said calmly. I can snatch the stone away before they get it, he thought. We must outrun them and get down the steps to my blade. Once I have the blade, the odds will be against them.

He reached into his pocket and withdrew the stone and held it out. "The girl," he said, opening then closing his hand. He sensed the mask of sadness on his face.

The bandits gasped when they saw the size of the perfectly oval stone with uncountable facets. They knew it was the Saqa crystal. Mars had sent them for it. Eelin was sure of that.

The troll moved his saber from Annah's back and she stepped toward Eelin. He stretched his hand to Annah's. In a flash the trolls brought out daggers, and the leader's saber was once again pressed into Annah's back. She screamed.

Eelin had no choice. He must give up the stone.

He tossed the stone to the floor and at the same time grabbed Annah's hand. The stone slid across the smooth floor, and Eelin heard the muttering of curses as the stone fell into a fissure. Annah snatched her cloak in a fluid movement and leapt away from the trolls' reach and into Eelin's arms.

"Run!" Eelin raced down the corridor pulling Annah with him.

Eelin and Annah flew down the temple stairs. Eelin grabbed Salt's strap and all three bounded toward Longdeg Caves. It seemed unbearably far off. "Curse my short legs," Eelin muttered.

Two of the bandits reached them before they had advanced fifty paces.

"Do not look back, Annah. Go!" Eelin commanded. He had unsheathed his sword and had slapped Salt's backside. Annah ran and Salt trotted behind her.

Eelin turned toward the two trolls who were just a breath away. They looked surprised to see Eelin's nicon blade brandished in outstretched hands.

The trolls held daggers that were useless against the fine sword. They split up and one of the them darted behind Eelin.

Eelin spun, feigning a jab at the troll behind him, then quickly leapt at the troll in front and thrust out his sword. He made a small wound to the troll's side. Then, without turning around, he reached behind and jabbed his blade outward and upward with all his might. The blade pierced the troll through the neck. The troll gasped and fell to the ground. Purple blood spurted from his wound. The other troll retreated inside the temple, clutching his ribs.

The fallen troll had a mortal wound, there was no doubt of it. Eelin stared at the body. "Soulless creature," he muttered. He had never killed another troll; he'd taken life only in the hunt for food. He was surprised at the anger that consumed him with ferocity. "I am a Prince, how dare they?" he said. But then, a moment later, he felt remorse for the kill. "Blessed be the gods for my strength," he offered reverently.

He glanced around and saw that all was clear. He cleaned his sword on the dead one's sash and ran to catch up with Annah.

"Oh, they got the stone!" Annah sobbed, when Eelin found her. "And it's all my fault. I shouldn't have…"

"We will get it back," Eelin said, though he doubted his words. "At least you are safe."

"But I'll never get home now," Annah said, crying harder. "I'll live here forever."

"No use crying," Eelin said. "It will not change anything." His head was spinning, and he felt weak in all his bones. He had killed his first troll and lost the precious crystal, all in a matter of a few heartbeats.

He patted his trouser pocket where the crystal had been. There was no feeling in that leg, nor in the hand that touched the pocket. He felt confusion of thought.

"No," he said. "Nothing has changed."

Annah's reached her hand to his and he felt better. "I will be all right," he said. He took a deep breath. He looked at his belt and pouches. The ruby knife was gone, the blade he was given at birth. He peeked inside the small yellow pouch at his belt. "Well," he said, with a weak smile, "they did not get the flint, or the precious Saqa seed. As long as I carry the seed, they have no chance of making a new Way." He said this with all the truth he could muster, but it was for Annah's benefit. The truth was that they might indeed have a seed somewhere. Mars or Rud, or both. He closed the little pouch and patted it. He smiled. Mars's minions did not get the lock of Annah's hair.

· SEVEN ·

Annah held tight to the fur tuft at Salt's neck as she climbed the road that pointed to the region of Barden. Salt's leather lead was loosely wrapped around her wrist like a bracelet.

As she walked, she could still feel the sting of the dagger on her spine and wondered if her skin had been cut or if she was bleeding. She felt no wet trickle of blood down her back. I will look later, she told herself. Her thoughts then returned to something which had been plaguing her for many hours: the image of Eelin's face, crestfallen, as he tossed the crystal to the floor. She had read the fear that shadowed his face. He was just as frightened as I was, she thought. Yet, despite Eelin's fear he had slain one of the bandits and scared off the other one. This is what bravery must be, she thought. She found herself staring at him and wanting to understand this creature who had saved her life, risking his own. Her fear of Eelin had gone for good.

She stroked Abbi's black cloth shoe that poked out of Salt's saddlebag. The doll comforted her, and made her think of Seton House, which now seemed unbearably far away, like an old memory that has faded to a single, fleeting image, and one wonders if the memory ever existed at all. I <u>will</u> get home, she promised bravely. Eelin said so.

Eelin walked a foot-stride ahead of Annah. His cloak billowed out behind him like a black cloud. The hilt of his sword glowed deep red as he carried it in his outstretched arm.

"What if they come back, an army of them, who aren't after jewels, but our heads?" Annah asked.

"Mars sent them," Eelin said, ignoring her question. He looked back at her and Annah saw that his mouth was curled into a snarl.

"Mars?" Annah said.

"My brother."

"Are you certain, Eelin?"

He turned to her with an arrogant look that Annah did not like. "What trolls would dare rob a Prince? And where did they get that fine saber of nicon?" Eelin said. His short legs climbed the hill easily, and Annah watched as his breath billowed out in a white vapor, cutting the air like a knife through a sheet of pale red gauze. "I will have his teeth," he said through deep breaths. "His teeth!"

"I can't understand why your own brother would betray you," Annah said.

"It is a long story," Eelin said. "He doubtless knew all along that I could not kill you." His voice softened. "Yet how could he know for certain? I have never revealed my deepest thoughts to him."

"You never intended to kill me?" Annah asked.

"I did not say that," Eelin said firmly. "But when the time came I could not do it. When I saw you..." There was a long pause. "Perhaps I never intended to kill you. I thought I could. I wanted to." He looked at her with apologetic eyes. "And that is the truth."

"Well, I'd always heard that trolls kill all the humans they see."

"Forget your childhood stories, Annah. You are here now, and you will know what is truth and what is not." In a queer voice he said, "And so will I. After I left the Hall, Mars must have gone straight to the passageway, taken the crushed flower, and searched the ground looking for bits of dust, for the remains of the crystal when the flower died. The rock I crushed would have confused him, but not finding the seed would confirm his suspicions that I took the stone. Yet I did not think he could summon help so quickly. I wonder if he has told Rud? I hope not."

"What do you think he will do with the stone?" Annah asked, biting her lip.

"He will, as Tye prescribes, make a new passageway to entice a human. He will kill the human that comes forth. Then he will have the Chair. That is all," Eelin said. "Perhaps he will wait until Rud is dead, but he will do the task in time. It will take some doing to find the way to grow the flower, I suspect. He may ask Rud's help. That is the part of this I cannot be sure about—whether or not he will seek my father's help to grow a new flower. But who knows? He may go to the Chronicler and kill her for the knowledge."

"And?"

"We must hurry. Because Mars knows our whereabouts. We are in tremendous danger. And so it will be until we reach Iteria."

"Why wouldn't Mars just come to Iteria and kill us?" Annah asked, taking long strides next to him.

"I doubt he would risk war with the other kingdom," Eelin said. "Unless he is more foolish than I thought. We planned to join the kingdoms as one when I took the Chair." He paused. "The Iterians are many. They are peaceful and will not allow killing on their soil. Especially killing humans." He chuckled. "Now killing me is another story. Mave would not mind getting rid of me."

"She hates you too?"

"She does not feel strongly about me one way or the other," he said in an offhand way.

"Why does everybody want to kill around here?" Annah asked, shaking her head in disgust.

"Is there no killing in your world?" He didn't wait for an answer. "It goes back ten thousand seasons," Eelin said. "Be assured that when I am king, there will be no more killing. <u>If</u> I am king."

Annah looked at him, Prince Eelin, a troll in human clothing. His shirt was stained with blood. The belt at his waist was finely tooled, stitched with perfectly spaced leather string. He knew how to wield a sword. He seemed more a warrior than a prince, especially now that he was without his jeweled necklace.

Annah looked at his left hand, the hand that held the sword in a strong grip. On the middle finger was a wide black ring. The bandits had probably not noticed it because it was the same color as the hairs on his finger.

"They didn't get your ring," she said kindly.

"Hmm? Oh, that." Eelin held up his fist. "No, they didn't get the ring." He lifted his hand to meet Annah's eyes.

Am I to kiss the ring? she wondered.

He withdrew his hand and admired the band.

"It's very nice," Annah said.

"It belonged to my mother. She wanted me to have it when she died."

Annah took his hand and brought it close again. The ring looked as though it was cut from a pipe of black stone. Etched into the stone were gold letters. Annah twisted the ring and read the tiny inscription: "The murky caverns speak, deep-throated, and are answered by the sweet breath of ocean and whisper of sky, and..."

"...Both are understood," Eelin finished.

Annah stared at Eelin. "Where did you get this ring?" she asked. "I have heard these words before, a poem written in my world, long ago. It's called Ode to a Troll."

"From Hela, I told you," Eelin said.

"And where did she get it?"

"It was a gift. From her father who was given it by a human. My mother had high regard for humans though it is said she knew only one: the birth maid at Mars's beginning.

After Hela died, the human woman told Rud that if Hela had been given human medicines she would have lived."

"Oh, I'm sorry."

"Father had the birth maid killed."

Annah winced. "You are so different from your father."

"Yet so much like him," Eelin said. The color seemed to drain from his eyes. "I am a troll. To many humans I am no better than vermin. That is what my father said."

"It's because they don't know you," Annah said.

Eelin smiled faintly. A stream of water fell from above and he wiped his hand across his forehead and pushed his hair away from his eyes. "We will be coming to the Longdeg Caves," he said. "It will be dark again soon."

Annah pulled the cloak around her as a reaction to the word dark. "I wish I could see in the dark," she said.

"I wish I could see in the sunlight," Eelin said. "How I wish..."

· EIGHT ·

Eelin watched as Annah yawned. "Just after Longdeg we will sleep," he said, turning away slightly, but still watching her out of the corner of his eye. "When we reach Atold."

"All right."

Longdeg Caves was never without a fine brown mist, created by the blood of animals mixed with water, splashing down in fine droplets. Annah cannot know this, Eelin thought in a protective way; her own blood was only recently spared. He pulled his cloak around his wide chest to keep the moisture off his shirt.

The end of the winding caves was near, marked by torches in the widening walls, heralding Atold.

The journey these last lengths had become a gradual slope downward and now the cave opened to reveal a deep sunken bowl, as though the earth was scooped out with a massive saber.

Beyond Atold were the hills of Barden, black mounds, opening the way to Iteria.

"Come Salt," Eelin said to the mule. He slapped her rump.

The lights of Atold blinked like eyes opening and shutting. The village was enclosed by a high wall of granite, and the dwellings were made of stone set into clay and were neatly arranged around the central forge. Perhaps two dozen Atolds lived here, Eelin thought. This part of his kingdom he rarely visited. In fact he had been here only twice in his lifetime. The high walls had a way of saying "Privacy," and privacy was respected, though he often thought of the area's forge and its remarkable iron tools, and weapons of finest nicon. The smell of burning metal stung the air.

Annah began to cough. She covered her face with her cloak as they made their way downhill toward the village.

Eelin touched her arm. His eyes roamed the village lights. "Here would be a good place for replacing my dagger," he said. The glow of phosphorescent rocks lighted the path now, leading up to the iron gates.

"You must not be recognized, Annah. Keep your cloak to your face just as it is now," Eelin said, pulling his own coarse cloak to him. "Look down. And don't worry, I will get you a bed at the inn, and hot food."

"A bed!" Annah said. "Oh, thank you."

"I doubt it is what you are used to," Eelin said. He slid his sword into the iron scabbard tied to Salt's back and covered the scabbard with the blanket. "Not a word about who I am," he told Annah, pulling her hair down into her face. He picked up brown dirt and rubbed it into her hair. "The color of your hair needs to be more like earth," he said. "You must pass for a troll."

Annah smiled, and rubbed some of the dirt from her hair across her forehead.

"That will be enough," Eelin said. "You are supposed to be troll, not dungrat."

They came to the gates and Eelin lifted the iron knocker and it fell with a deep groan. The gates had rusted to a powdery gold. Iron had a way of looking like gold after time, especially in a lantern's glow.

A small lookout door popped open, and a pair of eyes peered out. "Who are you, and what is your business in Atold?" a male voice boomed, sounding as metallic as the door.

"Food and lodging, my friend," Eelin said politely. "I have silver coin." The robbers did not get the purse at my ankle, Eelin thought, though there was not much coin there. I am a prince, what need have I to carry more than token coin? he told himself. I could use coin now. I must indeed look like a beggar, unless one sees the nicon sword strapped to Salt's back, the sword-hilt that carries the royal fire crest. I feel so far away from the princely life, he thought sadly. Now that Mars has the crystal, I might as well be a soulless beggar.

The gate creaked open finally and the gatekeeper shook a metal box. "Five and three," he said.

"Five and three," Eelin repeated, dropping two coins into the hole at the top of the box.

"Come Lalit," he told Annah, nodding to her. He took Salt's strap in his hand and they entered the village.

"Lalit?" Annah asked with a grin.

Eelin smiled.

The ground was paved with round red stones and many of the buildings had been decorated with the same stones pressed into the walls. The shops on either side of the road were topped with dwellings.

"That, I think, is the inn," Eelin said, pointing to a simple clay structure in the middle of the row of shops. He recognized the roof with its four chimneys. A porch of wood had been erected in the front, and on the porch sat two leather chairs. Across the road stood a forge where three males toiled behind the blazing fire. Smoke unfurled in great yellow ribbons, and floated up into the air.

A female and her two children scurried across the road in front of them, headed toward the forge. The younger of the trolls watched Annah with curious eyes until Eelin glared at him.

"Salt, come now," Eelin said crisply, and soon they had tied the mule to the granite post outside the inn. Eelin wrapped his arm around Annah and they climbed the steps.

"We need shelter," Eelin said to the white-haired innkeeper behind the stone counter.

There was an eating table in front of the fireplace and a cook's room beyond the arched doorway. Eelin's nose caught the odor of game stew.

In another corner of the room was a marble table where two elder male trolls sat gambling. Playing stones and bones, Eelin noticed.

The innkeeper shuffled around the counter and said, "Lodging for six rotations, eh?"

"Yes," Eelin said quietly. He did not think he would be recognized, still he kept his voice soft to disguise it. "We are on our way to Haza to visit relatives." It's only a half lie, Eelin thought. I do have relatives in Haza.

"This way," the innkeeper said, leading them outside and around the back of the inn. He led them past a tuber garden, past a pond where brown flowers floated, and across a courtyard to a small structure with a wooden door. Around his waist hung a leather cord, with two keys dangling from it. He took a key, unlocked the door and opened it, and turned to Eelin.

"This will do," Eelin said without so much as glancing inside. "Thank you."

The innkeeper hobbled away, grumbling something about dinner being late.

Eelin and Annah ducked as they entered the low doorway. Eelin took the key from the door and handed it to Annah and said, "I will unpack Salt. "Stay here, and do not open the door for any reason."

"Unless it's you," Annah said through gray wool.

Eelin grinned. "I'll return with food and drink."

And with that he left. He heard the door close and the key turn in the lock. He came around to the front of the inn. Salt was busy flicking her tail at the black moths that swirled near her. She breathed hard, snorting like Rud when he's angry, Eelin thought.

"Salt," he said gently, stroking her nose, and she laid back her ears. He bent over and began to unhook the large saddlebag, and then stopped. He had a better idea. *I'll bring Salt, bags and all, to the back. The beast can be tethered behind the room and I'll bring in the supplies.* He reached out to untie the leather strap.

"Hold!" a deep voice cried, pushing a blade into Eelin's spine. "You are Prince Eelin and you are hereby accused of treason."

· NINE ·

Eelin drew his sword in an instant. He whipped around and jabbed the blade at an invisible enemy.

"Who is there?" he demanded. He felt shame for not having been more alert.

A voice boomed from behind the stone porch column, "Friend or foe?"

"Friend or foe," Eelin repeated. The troll was youthful, Eelin could tell, despite the deep tone of the voice.

"Show yourself," Eelin demanded. "Or you will be turned to stew."

"As you command, my Lord," the voice said playfully. From behind the column a head popped out, showing a cap of wild black hair.

Eelin stared. There was something familiar about the hair that grew every direction from the rather pointed head. "Jaden?" he asked at last.

"In the body!" Jaden jumped out from behind the post and stood solidly on the ground, grinning. He sheathed his dagger and flung out his arms. "Eelin," he said happily, his voice pitched higher than it was a moment ago. He wore all black and was as dusty and disheveled as any troll Eelin knew.

Eelin rammed the sword into its scabbard still lashed to the mule. His mouth curled into a wide smile. They embraced. "Jaden! Such good luck it is to see you. It has been a thousand rotations, it seems, since we last spoke. And what brings you here?"

"Adventure, what else?" Jaden said in his usual gregarious way. "And you?"

"I best take you to the room so we can talk," Eelin said in a hushed voice. "Tell no one you have seen me and wait here while I take the beast to the back dwelling. Get us food and drink, will you? And be good enough to pay for it."

Jaden laughed, but did as he was told. Eelin led the mule around to the rear of the sleeping room. He patted Salt's head, looking kindly into her pink eyes. "Don't eat too much," he told her. He gave her a bag of seeds and waited patiently until she had devoured them. Then he returned to the inn to help Jaden.

Eelin did not realize how hungry he was until he saw the cook bring out the food and drink. There was stew made of river fowl, and tuber scented with mint oil, and steaming tea of exotic barkroot, warm ale, and roundbread, crisp on the edges and dripping with hot fat. And of course mushrooms, sweet and succulent, rolled in spices and baked on the hearth.

Eelin and Jaden carried the food on two iron trays.

"What is wrong, friend?" Jaden asked once they had rounded the back of the inn.

"You will see," Eelin said, trying to contain his emotions. When they reached the room he tapped on the door and said softly, "It's me."

The door opened and out popped a head of dirty hair wrapped in gray wool. One cautious eye regarded them.

"It's all right, Annah," Eelin said. "I have brought food and a friend."

Annah stepped back as Eelin and Jaden entered the room.

Eelin watched as Jaden stood silent, looking at Annah. She stared back, loosening the hood that framed her face.

Jaden and Eelin set the trays down on a low eating bench and Jaden put out his hand and said reverently, "Welcome, Annah." They clasped hands and he said, "I am honored to see you, my first human."

"She is Annah, and he is Jaden," Eelin said. He felt proud to be the first to introduce Jaden to a human. The fact that she seemed to be so close to their own age and wisdom made her especially wondrous.

Annah removed her cloak and laid it across one of the feather-stuffed sleeping pads, while Eelin went out to unload Salt. He returned with the bags and set them down on a bench near the door. He leaned his sword against the door and locked the door with the key.

Jaden arranged the food on the stone eating bench, where fire danced in an iron bowl.

Eelin told Annah, "Jaden is my closest friend and the best swordsman and long knife-thrower in all of Haza, and Iteria for that matter."

"Taught him all he knows of swordsmanship," Jaden said light-heartedly.

Eelin tossed his cloak on the sleeping pad next to Annah's. "Sit now." He plopped down on the floor in front of the table and breathed in the odor of the steaming food. "Let us eat and share stories of what brings us here." He looked sideways at Jaden. "I'll bet my story is better than yours."

"I hope so," Jaden said. He paused, looking at the food. "I have no coin left."

"We will survive," Eelin said. Kneeling, he spooned up stew into three steel bowls. He smiled at Annah, and gestured for her to sit next to him.

Jaden shook his head at Eelin. "What a brave soul <u>you</u> are! To travel with a human..."

Eelin shrugged. "All part of being a prince, I suppose."

"You are in constant danger."

"I realize this, yes."

"And it just so happens I'm looking for danger."

"Do you seek employment?" Eelin asked impishly. He set his tea mug down with a clatter.

"What kind of employment?" Jaden asked with a smile.

"Travel with us to Iteria, and help ward off bandits and magic most evil."

"Iteria? Yes, that is where I would take a human if I found one," Jaden said thoughtfully.

Eelin nodded at Annah. "Do you remember me telling you that there are others like me who share my feelings for humans? Jaden is one such troll."

"Have you the stone?" Jaden asked suddenly.

Annah spoke up. "No," she said. "It was stolen."

Jaden grimaced. "Not good at all."

Eelin said, "It is my own fault."

"No, it's my fault," Annah cut in. "I wanted to go inside the temple at Thenon. The bandits were hiding there."

"They would have found us in or outside of the temple," Eelin said to console her. "They were waiting for us and knew exactly what they were looking for."

"Mars, perchance?" Jaden raised an eyebrow. He washed down bread with a gulp of ale.

Eelin patted his hip. "They got my knife."

"Easily replaced," Jaden said. "Here in Atold you can get anything, for a price."

"Another problem," Eelin said. "I didn't think to bring coin. I can pay for lodging, but that is all."

Jaden replied, "I can barter. Wait! The forgesmith owes me a favor." His eyes narrowed to black lines and his sharp teeth flashed. "We'll have you a better blade than the one that was stolen. Of course there won't be rubies on it, or that fancy royal fire crest." He smiled slyly. "But it will be sharp as Mave's tongue..."

Eelin grinned. "And true as her heart."

Eelin exploded in laughter and didn't stop until his ribs ached. Jaden laughed hard too, snorting and slapping his thighs.

"Well then it is settled," Jaden said at last, pounding his fist on the table. "I will take your offer of employment at a cost of, hmmm…" He dismissed things with a wave of the hand. "We shall settle later." He quaffed the rest of his ale, wiped his mouth across his sleeve, and announced, "By the gods, I promise to protect you and Annah on your journey to Iteria."

"Good," Eelin said, clapping him on the shoulder. "Good."

Jaden bowed his head and closed his eyes. "And may the gods protect us, because we will surely need it."

· TEN ·

Annah had eaten ravenously before stretching out on one of the dense feather pads that lay on the stone floor. She closed her eyes and when next she opened them, Eelin and Jaden were slipping away. She awoke sometime later to hear them as they returned. She had no idea how long they had been gone, but she was so tired she promptly fell back to sleep. It had been the first good sleep since coming to this foreign world. Why was I chosen? she asked herself, in the throes of sleep.

Later she awoke, refreshed, to see Eelin and Jaden stretched out on the floor, snoring away, with their swords lying crossed between them. It was as if they had set them like that as some sort of pre-sleep ritual. Next to Eelin's hand lay a dagger in a silver scabbard. The hilt was blackest iron, crude compared to the blade that was taken. Annah was glad he had been able to replace it.

Drawing her knees up, she sat and drank earthy-tasting tea warmed by candle. I suppose it's morning somewhere," she murmured, looking into the yellowish tea. "That is what I miss the most," she whispered. "Time." She felt as though she were suspended in space, swinging from a wire, never knowing where she was, but constantly moving toward something that was just out of reach.

Seton House was fading from her thoughts so quickly. She could no longer picture the color of the room where she had spent her days reading to the children, helping them to hold chalk as they wrote the alphabet on their small blackboards. Was the room pale orange, or pale yellow? The children's faces were beginning to blur in her memory. It's because so much has happened to me, she thought. I'm losing touch with my own world with each passing moment.

She looked at Eelin and Jaden, asleep, vulnerable, like children. She could easily escape. She studied Eelin's long braids. He turned over and she looked at his closed eyes, with the lashes straight and black. She looked carefully at him and at Jaden. They were so different from what she had expected trolls to look like. She watched Eelin's eyes as they twitched in dreams. His full lips curled into a smile, then retreated into a pout, then became a straight line. His face was full of small hairs, but they were soft. She thought there might be a dimple in his chin.

    She had seen the drawings in history books of the prehistoric man that trolls and humans were said to had evolved from. Eelin and Jaden resembled the prehistoric man more than present-day humans did; it was as though trolls had been frozen in time. But she supposed she had grown used to their look because as she watched them sleep, she found herself smiling. There was something familiar and good about them.

ಲ೦ಬಾ

Annah took her place between Jaden and Eelin as they stole through the village. All was silent. No fires burned in the forges.

Eelin carried Salt's lead in one hand, and his other hand rested on the hilt of his knife. He seemed more confident now that he carried a hip blade. He seemed to stand taller. His double-edged sword had been tightly wrapped and tied to Salt, along with fresh provisions courtesy of Jaden's quick tongue.

Jaden wore his sword at his back, the silver hilt yellow in the lights that pointed to the village gate. He took long strides while Eelin crept like a cat, his cloak wrapped tightly around him.

Jaden was dark-skinned and short and solid, and quick to smile. His trousers were frayed at the bottom and the pockets were bulging, except for the back pocket that had been torn off. His shirt was in the same condition as his pants, though Annah could tell it was well-made.

Eelin was neat and meticulous, his shirt washed of blood stains, and even the nails on his fingers were clean and carefully filed to smooth points. Annah thought when she first saw him that he was hideous and filthy, and now she found him interesting. Has he changed, or have I? she wondered. Has he become more human? Will I become like a troll?

The idea was not so far-fetched; already she could feel something happening to her eyes. It was not that she was learning to see in the dark, as Eelin had predicted, but when the light was there, it bothered her eyes. The yellow torch lights of Atold burned a little too bright, and she shielded her eyes as she passed by them.

Annah pulled her cloak to hide her face as Jaden bid good-life to the gatekeeper.

Once they were a fair distance from the gate, Jaden pulled out his sword and sparred with an invisible partner. His blade was like a bolt of lightning as it cut through the air. He reached up and sheathed his sword into the scabbard at his back. Then he began a story that seemed to go in circles, something about a sword that kept bending and becoming useless whenever it was used for bad purposes.

Eelin, on the other hand, seemed lost in serious thought.

They are opposites, Annah thought. Complete opposites.

Eelin had paid for the room at the inn. Jaden had had asked for a free parcel of bread and cheese for the journey, saying he deserved it for the time he once defended the innkeeper's wife from a ruffian bloated with tuber ale. Eelin had laughed and said, "You never give up, do you, Jaden?" The innkeeper had shook his head, but his wife had caught Jaden's roguish grin, and in the end Jaden had come away with more food than he had asked for. Eelin said the innkeeper was fearful that if he didn't oblige, Jaden would talk him to death.

As the three of them walked, Eelin and Jaden spoke to each other in half-sentences, punctuated by grunts and growls, and words that were in a language Annah did not recognize. When they laughed they slapped their thighs and snorted. Jaden's laugh was loud, and Annah found herself laughing too, though she did not understand much of what was being laughed about. Eelin's high-pitched laugh came like music, and Annah felt glad that he was able to relax. The name "Mave" came up quite a bit, which always brought at least a snicker from Eelin and Jaden.

The thought of Jaden as a protector made Annah giggle. The bandits from here to Iteria will know we are coming as long as Jaden stays with us, she thought, for they will hear us. Still, he knows how to wield a sword, there is no denying that. And he made the time pass quickly with his entertaining stories and jokes, even if much of what he said made no sense. Troll humor was very different from human humor. Annah caught part of a joke about the old troll woman who had barbberry pie on her teeth and when she kissed her children they said, "Ho, barbberry!"

Many times along the way Eelin and Jaden lowered their voices to whispers, and Annah once again caught the word "Mave." During these talks Annah busied herself by scratching Salt's soft ears and feeding her the grain Jaden had "borrowed" from the inn. She patted Abbi's poor mutilated hand. She wished she had brought Abbi's red gloves, but they were tucked away in the drawer of the dresser that stood in her corner of the dormitory.

She began collecting pretty stones she found on the ground, putting them into the pocket of her dress. Some of the stones were so smooth and shiny they could be used as jewelry. One of the rocks she picked up was laced with amber and reminded her of a calico cat. There was a deep red spot in the center, like a drop of blood. The stone would be worth something back home, she was sure.

"I know some magic," Jaden announced as they crossed a damp geyser plain. The clouds were rolling in, and they were the color of pea soup. Barden was close now, Eelin said, and Annah thought its mountains looked like jagged purple shadows against the distant cavern walls.

Jaden turned to Annah and grinned. "I can make things disappear," he said.

Eelin rolled his eyes. "Easy task in these clouds."

Annah said, "What kind of things?"

Jaden touched Abbi with his fingertip. "Your toy. I can make that disappear."

"But can you make it reappear?" Eelin asked, chuckling.

"Of course I can," Jaden said, bowing. "The Wizard can do anything."

"Then bring back the Saqa stone," Eelin said.

Jaden made a face. "Let me see your doll, Annah, and I'll show you," he said eagerly.

"Why don't you make something of *yours* disappear, like your sword?" Annah said, clutching Abbi's leg tightly. "She's already missing two fingers, and I don't think I want to lose the rest of her, thank you very much."

"Very well," Jaden said, reaching back and whisking his sword from its scabbard. "The blade it is." They all stopped in their tracks as he held the sword in his outstretched hands. He closed his eyes. "Wisdom of the earth, fire and souls, come together in these hands."

Eelin yawned.

Nothing happened.

Jaden took a deep breath and repeated the incantation. The sword began to glow red hot and then it quivered, as though caught in the shimmer of afternoon sun. Annah kept an eye on Jaden's hands because she had been told that magicians have quick hands. But when the sword slowly went out of focus and disappeared right before her eyes, she gasped.

"Where did it go?" she asked. She pulled back the hood of her cloak and stared at Eelin.

Eelin smiled and shrugged his shoulders.

Jaden opened one eye. "If you're nice to me, I'll tell you where it went," he said.

Annah reached out to touch his outstretched hands, and he took a giant step backward.

Eelin laughed.

Jaden was chanting again, eyes closed. Slowly the sword reappeared in his hands. He snapped opened his eyes and grinned. "Worked well," he said.

"All right, tell me how you did it," Annah begged.

At last Jaden said, putting his sword away, "the sword didn't disappear. I simply willed your eyes blind to it."

Annah furrowed her brow. "Could you see the sword?" she asked Eelin.

"Yes," he answered. "And if you had reached out, you would have felt the metal in his hands."

"Where did you learn that trick?" Annah wanted to know.

"I learned from a wise old man," Jaden replied, grinning at Eelin. "A wizard."

"A wizard," Annah repeated. "Could you teach me some magic?"

"It takes a lot of practice," Jaden said. "It took me a lifetime."

Eelin shook his head. "This is the simplest of tricks. An infant can do this magic. It is not even magic at all."

"Then why can you not do it?" Jaden asked him.

"I'd like to learn," Annah interrupted, tugging on his ragged sleeve. "Please teach me."

"I'd be happy to teach you," Jaden promised. "But Fally himself can teach you that, and more, when we reach Iteria." He smiled wryly at Eelin. "Mave's Grandfather."

"We are halfway there now," Eelin said, suppressing a grin.

"Maybe if we are attacked by robbers you can make us all disappear," Annah suggested, and Eelin and Jaden burst into laughter. Annah laughed too.

Their laughter faded when Eelin put his finger to his lips and whispered, "Did you hear that? Someone is following us." He dropped Salt's lead and reached for the blanket roll. His blade was out in a moment, and Jaden unsheathed his blade as well.

Annah's heart burned in her chest. From behind them came a snarl, and she spun around, as did Eelin and Jaden, to see a black-cloaked figure ducking behind a rock 100 feet away. The figure was enormous, tall as two people end to end.

She rubbed her eyes. She could have sworn the figure had two heads.

· ELEVEN ·

The moment Eelin saw the two-headed creature his deepest fears were confirmed. Not only had Mars sent the bandits for the Saqa crystal, but now he was sending a Duot to finish them off. "This is war," he muttered, "war, when my brother sends a Duot from the army I should rightfully command." He fought the urge to scream out his brother's name in hatred. He wished that Annah was not present so that he could freely curse.

Jaden began to push Annah toward a dark cave mouth near a bubbling geyser. "Safety there," he told her.

"But I won't be able to see," Annah said in a desperate voice. She stood frozen.

"No time," Jaden snapped.

"Wait," Eelin said. He quickly sheathed his sword and fetched the candle from Salt's pack. He took the flint from the belt pouch and scraped the flint across a rock with one hand, while the other hand gathered up a small nest of leaves from the ground. A spark ignited the leaves and he blew on the spark gently. In a flash the candle was lit. With heaving breath, he gave the candle to Annah. "Go. Now!"

"But..." she said.

"Take care to shelter it from the wind with your hand. To the cavern." He was snarling now, and she quickly ran off.

Eelin, sword in hand, moved toward the boulder where the creature was last seen. Jaden moved next to him. Their swords were almost identical—nickel, iron, and carbon—except that on the hilt of Eelin's sword blazed rubies in the shape of fire.

Jaden whispered, "I've never battled a Duot." His tone was one of caution and excitement.

"Nor I," Eelin said, feeling perspiration crawl down the back of his neck.

"This is Mars's fatal mistake," Jaden muttered, all the humor gone from his voice.

"He would have me killed," Eelin said sadly. "I didn't want to believe..." and he couldn't finish. At that moment he knew he had no brother.

They stopped to listen, both of them with cocked heads. There came no sound from behind the huge rock. Eelin knew the creature was capable of using magic, though the magic was crude and would not last long. If he kept his attention fixed on the spot where he knew the creature was hiding, eventually his keen ears would detect the presence, even if the creature was invisible to his eyes. The creature had made itself invisible. That much he knew.

"Jaden, do you see the Duot?" he whispered.

"No, my Prince."

The magic was not so crude after all, to make two trolls blind.

Eelin looked down at the ground and saw footprints, thin and long-toed, and the footprints went in two directions: toward the boulder and toward—

He whipped his head around and stared at the cave where they had sent Annah. Had the Duot changed its mind and followed Annah? Duots cannot move too quickly, and they most certainly cannot be in two places at once. Unless there are two of them.

He motioned for Jaden to keep still while he darted across the plain toward the cave. As he ran he listened and searched the green air for ripples, for wind; he tried to feel changes in temperature. The creature's magic cannot last much longer, he told himself; it will have to show itself soon. Had it already entered the cave?

Eelin ran faster, with his sword swinging wildly in front of him, slashing through the mist. He fought the urge to shout a war whoop to turn the creature away from Annah. What if it had already found her, and was at this moment tearing her head from her shoulders? He could not bear to think of it.

He stepped into the dark cave. There was no candle light. Sorrows, he thought. It's my fault. I should have kept her by my side. He stood just inside the cave's entrance, watching the walls. The cave was round, except for a low hall that spoked off the back, leading to the sleeping room. The cave had belonged to a troll family once, he knew by the pictures painted on the rock walls. He lifted his nostrils. There was no smell of blood. Relief. But the creature was here. He could hear its breath as it exhaled.

The cave's darkness gave him luck since Duots cannot see without some light. Eelin tried not to think of the possibility that the candle had gone out when Annah was taken.

He approached the sleeping room. Peering in he saw was Annah, huddled in the back corner with her legs drawn up tight and her head down. Then she disappeared, hidden by the Duot's shadow. In the next moment she reappeared, but only partially: the corner of her frock and part of her right shoulder. The Duot was standing over her. I may be blind to the creature but not its shadow, he thought.

He stole silently toward them with his sword in outstretched arm. He stopped when he was close enough to feel their warmth. He pulled back on the arm that held the sword and prepared to strike.

If the creature were too close to Annah, the sword would pierce her as well. He narrowed his eyes and said a quick prayer. Then, with all his strength, he plunged the blade halfway into the flesh it found. He heard no gasp, had no idea if the blade had sunk into a vital spot, and so he pulled it out, buried it in a lower spot of the body, and withdrew it. He jumped back just as a gush of air swiped at him—the creature's deadly talon, no doubt. But his sword had found soft organ, for now there came a horrific shriek.

The creature came into focus as the magic escaped it like air from lungs. It was indeed a two-headed Duot, with a slice to its upper back and a fatal gaping wound to its lower abdomen. It fell to the ground, rolling itself side to side and gasping for breath.

"Who sent you?" Eelin demanded of the monster. He touched his blade to the Duot's neck, at the point just before it branched off into two heads.

A growling, guttural sound came out of its throats, speaking words that were unintelligible. Both of its faces were twisted into a mask of pain and anger, and brown blood dribbled from the mouths. Four green bulging eyes stared vacantly. Its tattered cape lay limply around it like the broken wings of a bat.

"Who sent you?" Eelin repeated in a louder voice. The creature's stare did not change. But then there came a bolt of laughter, deep and sickening. And then the laughter stopped abruptly. It was finished.

Eelin stepped around the creature and gathered Annah to him and wrapped her cloak tightly around her.

"I was so frightened," Annah whispered through trembling hands that covered her face.

"You were lucky," Eelin said, holding her. "Duots are horrible, all of them. Thank the gods the creature could not readily see you."

"I felt something enter the cave," Annah said, breathless. "I knew something was here, though I couldn't see it. I blew out the candle. I thought maybe it—the Duot—wouldn't find me."

Eelin looked into her eyes that could not see him. "Are you saying you sensed the creature, even in its invisible realm?"

"Yes."

"Perhaps you have some magic of your own, girl."

At that moment Jaden dashed into the cave and stopped in front of the slain Duot. He stood heaving, clutching his sword, and it was smeared with dark blood. "Who is the master swordsman?" he asked Eelin. "You have struck with precision."

Eelin nodded at the dead creature. "You have taught me well, Jaden."

They stripped the creature of its dagger and of the sack of coins it wore at its side. The creature was one Eelin recognized from the Hall. He lit the candle and held it in front of Annah's eyes and she gasped.

"That's a Duot! Such a huge, ugly thing. Is it a troll?"

"The Duots are a two-headed race of trolls," Eelin replied. "They are the god's punishment. And Assassins in my father's army. They can be made to do anything. And they are none too bright."

"But they are fiercely strong and possess a little magic," Jaden added. "Enough to almost get you killed. There is another dead one yonder."

"We must be more cautious," Eelin said, "now that the Duots have come." He helped Annah to her feet.

Annah turned to him and her eyes found his. "We are going to die, aren't we?"

· TWELVE ·

Eelin touched Annah's arm and promised to protect her. It was good enough for now. I felt so helpless, she thought, with just a candle for protection. I would have felt safer with a sword. I could swing it and the creature couldn't have touched me. This is what she told herself, and she believed it.

She stepped around the dead Duot, feeling weak as she looked while Eelin brought the candle close to the two faces. She wondered what it would be like to have two heads, to look over and see a face staring back. Would you be able to hear each another's thoughts?

The Duot's heads were nothing alike; one head was ruddy and swollen and large-eared, while the other was thin and pinched with a pointed nose and nostrils the size of prunes. Both had bulging eyes which had rolled up into their sockets, showing white mapped with red veins.

Annah found herself staring. She had never seen death before. The two heads were turned away from each other, and the thick tongues hung out. The creature was ten feet tall easily.

"I'll go loot the other one," Eelin volunteered, turning to leave. "I must see what kind of blow the creature received." He paused a moment and grinned at Jaden. "I believe she has the magic."

Jaden smiled. "I knew it all along." He took Annah's arm and said, "We best be going now, human. If there are two, there are more coming."

Annah and Jaden left the cave and found Salt wandering near a distant geyser, nibbling yellow shoots.

Eelin soon came bearing an iron dagger and a bag of jingling coins. "No time to lose," he said. He loaded the mule with the things he had taken from the Duot.

Jaden led Salt down the road, and Eelin and Annah followed.

"I would like to have a sword as well," Annah said quietly. Her words surprised her. She'd never touched a sword in her life.

Eelin did not miss a step. "Of course," he said. "You can start with my own dagger, here, and we'll get you a proper blade in Sagpine."

He didn't even ask me whether I know how to use a sword, she thought with a little smile. "I'd feel safer with something," she went on.

"I understand," Eelin said. "It was foolish of me to have denied you a blade." He removed the scabbard from his belt and handed it to Annah. "We'll get you a belt as well." He took for himself the iron dagger that had belonged to the Duot, and shoved it under his belt. "Before the journey is over you might need to fight."

"By myself?" Annah asked, terrified.

"Perhaps," Eelin said in a serious voice. "But I will try very hard not to let that happen."

Annah rolled the silver scabbard over in her hand. It was heavy, and the hilt was still warm from Eelin's touch. She tucked the scabbard under her arm and withdrew the blade. It was frighteningly sharp to look at and she put it back. "I hope I never have to use this," she breathed, remembering the look of death on the Duot's faces, the look that could well be on her own face soon.

They continued on the road, stopping only once to eat a meal of bread and goat cheese. They soon came to a tunnel that was dusty and hot and so low they all had to duck. Annah coughed and perspired from the heat. As they made their way through the smoky darkness, her body's clock told her it was time for sleep. She yawned repeatedly until, next to her, Eelin said, "I too am tired. We can sleep soon." His words sounded unemotional, and Annah had the feeling that to Eelin, the word "soon" meant merely sometime in the future.

Soon the tunnel widened and dipped into a valley, and set down in the valley was a village. Lights glittered in windows. This looks like a human city, Annah thought, and she wondered if Eelin might be right about her getting used to the dark. She could make out some of the shapes of the dwellings, even the ones where no lights burned. If only there was a moon, she thought, glancing up at the black ceiling.

"Sagpine at last," Eelin told her.

They brought Salt down the steep trail. Salt was sure-footed, but Annah had trouble keeping from sliding.

"There, Salt," Jaden said, patting the mule's head. The mule nuzzled his hand and he laughed.

At last they reached the village and Jaden led the way through the winding main road.

Annah was entranced by the village. Rows of stone buildings lined the main street and lights burned in carved-out windows. All the buildings were small, as though inhabited by little people. The buildings were intricately painted with scenes from troll farming life. On every building burned a tiny yellow lantern and although there were only a dozen structures, their sameness gave the village a sense of belonging. What a quaint place, she thought as she noticed children sitting in circles playing. The girls wore frocks like the one she wore underneath her cloak. Their hair was braided like Eelin's, only without the gold thread woven through. They played a hand-clapping game and sang songs. Annah wished she could say hello to them. But that would be dangerous, so instead she wrapped her cloak tightly around her, pushed her hair in front of her eyes and pulled the hood down to her nose and looked down.

"They seem happy," Annah whispered.

"Midseason," Jaden said, turning his head to smile at her.

"What is midseason?" Annah asked.

"A celebration of the crop harvest," he replied. "Here in Sagpine they grow vegetables under the phosphorescent light of the fungus moss. Tubestalks and so on. They provide food for many families in Haza." He grinned. "The best tuber ale comes from this village. Ale-making is an important wisdom we learned from humans."

Eelin said, "That is why you like humans so much."

"True, true," Jaden said, chuckling.

"It is said many humans walked in Sagpine and left their wisdom," Eelin told Annah.

Annah could understand what he meant, she could feel their presence in the village. She felt comfortable here. She snuck peeks into dwellings as she passed by, peering through the windows. Before she knew it, she was lagging behind Eelin and Jaden. In one dwelling, the door stood open just a crack, and Annah stopped. From beyond the door came the faint odor of a recognizable spice. Was it cloves? Or nutmeg? She strained to look inside. Surely those spices were brought by humans.

Slowly she pushed the door open. Inside the cave was a small, comfortable-looking room with a stone fireplace where a fire burned. There were two leather chairs facing the fireplace. She gasped.

She stood paused for several moments, thinking about home, feeling tired, and wanting to sit down on one of the chairs. She stepped inside the room, keeping one foot on the threshold. She glanced around. On one of the walls stood a books shelf with rows and rows of books. "Oh! What a wonderful little room," she said aloud. I wish..."

She crossed the room and stepped closer to the books. She reached out to touch one of the spines, and all at once a bony hand clamped around her mouth. In her struggle to turn and break away she became entangled in her cloak.

A hairy face pressed next to hers, and warm breath tickled her ears. A hand stroked her face and then the breath sucked in. "Oh, I knew it! Greetings, human," a feeble voice whispered in her ear.

The hand released Annah and she spun to face an ancient troll with wispy white hair that trailed down to her waist, and in the candlelight it hung like white smoke. The old troll smiled and was almost toothless.

Instantly Annah's dagger was out of its scabbard. She stood breathless and terrified, waving the dagger in front of her.

"I haven't seen a human for such a long season," the old troll continued kindly, ignoring the knife. Her eyes were colorless, and vacant.

"What part of the human world are you from?" she asked. "Africa? New Zealand?"

"Let me go," Annah said, backing toward the door. "Or I will cut your gizzards out."

"You are free to go," the old troll said gently. "But I hope you will stay. I mean you no harm, girl. I merely seek stories of your world. Please, please, take a seat and tell me a quick story." She gestured to the chairs in front of the fireplace. Between the chairs stood a round table. The fire in the stone fireplace was small but bright. Annah wondered if she could sit for just a second. It wouldn't hurt…

At that moment Eelin and Jaden crashed into the room wielding swords.

"Stand away, old one!" Eelin commanded.

In one fluid movement Jaden had the troll's arms pinned behind her back. "Don't move, or death is yours," he said in a firm, deep voice.

"I have things under control," Annah said, showing her knife. "I don't believe the old troll meant me any harm." The troll was fragile, maybe even close to death. And there was something human about her.

"Perhaps, and perhaps not," Eelin said. He stepped closer to the troll woman, twisting his head to study the face.

"I was just talking to the human girl," the old troll said in a faltering voice, touching Eelin's cheek. "Please don't deny me the opportunity to gain wisdom of her world..." She sounded like she was about to cry.

Eelin sheathed his sword. "Release her, Jaden." He turned to Annah and smiled. "Annah, I would like you to meet the Chronicler."

· THIRTEEN ·

Eelin let the cloak fall from around him.

The Chronicler stepped so close to Eelin Annah thought she was going to kiss him. She reached out and touched his cheek.

A look of surprise crossed the Chronicler's face. "Eelin, my Lord!" she gasped, bowing low. "I am glad you have come, though I fear circumstances are grave to have brought you here." She turned to Annah. "My name is Winspur, and I am most glad to see you, dear girl."

Eelin bowed. "And I am most glad to make your acquaintance finally. I have heard much about you." His grin covered his face.

"I hope it was not all lies," Winspur said with a laugh. "Please, let us sit awhile." She pointed once again to the chairs at the fireplace. She turned toward Jaden and said, "You also, Jaden. I know your father…"

"It will have to be a short while, my friend," Jaden cut in.

Eelin sighed. "We have important business in Sagpine, and I'm afraid…" His voice trailed off. "And I had so many questions to ask you."

"And I Annah," Winspur said, smiling.

Eelin said, "Perhaps if there is time when we are finished we will speak, Chronicler."

Winspur nodded as she led Annah toward the fire with a hand on her shoulder. "Child, you do not have to hide under this cloth. You are safe here with me." She took Annah's cloak and hung it on a hook near the front door. "You are not the first human to cross this threshold, no indeed."

Eelin turned to go, but stopped at the door and said, "You have not, by any chance, seen my brother, have you?"

"Goodness no," Winspur said. "He could never find me. Only those I seek… Like Annah."

Eelin said, "Jaden and I will be back here in one-half rotation, yes?"

Winspur nodded, and Eelin and Jaden left.

"Would you like some tea, Annah?" Winspur asked as soon as they were gone.

Annah had just settled into the brown leather chair in front of the fireplace. "I surely would," she answered, letting her body go limp in the soft chair.

The old troll turned and trotted off. "I'll just be a moment," she called.

Annah let her gaze wander around the room. The fireplace was made of blackened bricks with a gray marble mantle. Above the mantle was a crude painting of a plump troll man. And of course there were the books. Despite her fatigue, she could not resist getting up from her seat to examine the books. The shelves that held them were made of an odd wood, dark yellow with a black pattern like leopard spots.

One shelf was dedicated to dictionaries and other reference books, in many languages. There was a whole row of books on botany and wildlife.

Annah moved to another section which contained nothing but fairy tales. "It's a library," Annah whispered. "Like at home." The books were in alphabetical order by title.

The Faeries' Dream was one of the titles. It was a tiny red leather book with gold script letters. Annah took it down from the shelf. On the cover of the book was embossed a delicate, winged fairy fluttering through a forest. She opened the book to the middle and began to read: "Once, when the moon fell from the sky, the Faery Queen was called to summon it back."

Annah returned the book. A large black book next to it was called *Frogham's Quest*. There was a series of seven books called *Troll Physiology and Lore*. Annah opened the first book of the series. The paper was so brittle it nearly crumbled in her hands. The book contained ink drawings of trolls, and there was an anatomical section showing bones and muscles. Annah read, "The troll brain, while complex compared with other subterranean species, seems incapable of mastering the task of reading." There were footnotes at the bottom of the page. Annah returned the book to its place.

On the spine in small letters was printed the author's name. It said, "S. Thigpen, Ph.D., M.D. Oxford."

"Ah, I see you have found my divine collection," Winspur said, padding into the room, carrying a tray.

Annah sat down. Winspur placed the tray on the little round table between the chairs. There were two cups of tea and one spoon, and a bowl of milk and a tiny cup of sugar. There were two white cookies on a silver plate. Winspur took her seat, smoothing her red robe.

"My books give me great pleasure," she said. "Sugar?"

"Yes, please."

Winspur stared at the books, trance-like. "Milk?"

"Yes, please."

Winspur fixed the teas, stirring them, and then she settled into the chair.

"Is it really true that trolls aren't able to read?" Annah asked.

Winspur smiled. "I am living proof that it is not true. However, it has taken me many seasons to learn what I know. I am one of the oldest students of this most difficult endeavor." She sipped tea and pointed to the round white cookies on the plate. "Please take one. I made them myself, from an authentic human recipe. Aunt Zane's Best Sugar Cookies," she said proudly. "It's not unlike your learning magic?"

"Magic?" Annah repeated.

"Reading for trolls is not unlike..."

"Oh, that, yes. Magic is hard to learn." She wondered how Winspur knew she was trying to learn magic.

"It seems the one wisdom humans wish to learn most from trolls," she said, as though reading Annah's mind.

Annah took a cookie, and it tasted a bit stale. "Just like the ones we make on holidays," she said politely. She sipped tea from a teacup with a delicate floral pattern and gold edging. Winspur's cup was of a different pattern with a chip in the handle.

"I've been saving the cookies in a tin," Winspur said. "For the occasion that a human would come to visit. It's been a while. I apologize." She grinned. "How is the tea? Is it all right?"

"It's perfect," Annah said. "Just like at home." The word home sounded strangely foreign.

"The tea came from England," Winspur went on. "Brought to me by my dear friend Clement."

"Is Clement a..."

"Oh yes, he is—was—a human. He passed on unfortunately." Winspur sighed.

"I'm sorry," Annah said. She pointed to the mantle. "And who is the troll in the painting?"

"My husband, my Garine," she replied, without looking at the painting. "I miss him. I miss them both terribly. Clement and me, we used to talk of books and of course the weather." She brightened. "But now that you are here..."

Annah shifted in her seat. "Well, if you must know, we're passing through on our way to Iteria. I really can't stay long." She dipped her cookie in her tea. "Mars has come after us, you know. He sent the Duots."

Winspur nodded. "I understand. Iteria will be safe." She held her tea cup to her lips for a moment before drinking, and the steam made beads of water on her nose, which was so long it nearly touched the liquid. "Unfortunate, that you are not safe here. Ah, for the old days." She leaned her head back in her chair and closed her eyes. A small smile curled on her wrinkled lips. "Once, there were many humans."

Annah nodded in understanding. "Yes, but then the humans brought disease, right?"

Winspur's eyes snapped open. "That is only part of it. The humans and trolls are innately different. Many factors, many reasons..."

"You seem human," Annah said. "I mean, you seem to know a lot about them. Us."

"I have studied humans for a lifetime. I am sad that we cannot live and thrive in each other's worlds."

"Why can't the trolls just go through the passageway and live with humans?" Annah asked. "I would never harm a troll..."

Winspur shook her head. "The sunlight is too bright for trolls. Blindness would surely come, if not death. It is well documented in Tye." Her face became faraway for a moment, then she smiled as though she had a secret. She lowered her voice and looked around. "But there are trolls who do not believe Tye. They believe trolls can live in the human world. They believe in magic not revealed in Tye. The ancient magic of the Saqa."

"The Saqa," Annah echoed. "It's the way home."

"It is known," Winspur continued, "that the ancient magic of Saqa can be found in a book."

"And where is the book?" Annah asked, biting her lip. "Because maybe it tells how we can make a new passageway and I can go..."

"Who knows?" Winspur said forlornly. "And yes, it holds all the magic. Of course, like Tye, it tells of the beginning, when humans and trolls lived as one race above ground. It tells of how a clan was cast underground, only to evolve in a different way from humans, to evolve as trolls. But the book also tells of the beginning of a wondrous flower called the Saqa. The trolls took the Saqa with them when they went below and the Saqa evolved along with the trolls. This was of course millions of your years ago. And," she said, "the book is said to show the way for trolls to live in sunlight..."

Annah cried out, "You could live in England if we could find the magic! We have to find this book. Before Mars does."

Winspur laughed. "It is said the book was destroyed. But I believe it is hidden somewhere, to keep trolls from leaving Haza. Because you see, Annah, if it were true that a troll could walk in the human world, what would prevent all the trolls from leaving? I certainly would not stay here, where the air is putrid fire."

"It would not be so bad, would it, for trolls to live with humans?"

"Not for me," Winspur said. "But if you were king, would you want your subjects to leave?"

"No, I suppose not." Annah looked into the troll's tired eyes. "It doesn't matter anyway, because the last passageway is closed."

Winspur smiled, showing purplish gums. "Mars has the crystal, yes?"

"Yes."

"I should have guessed when I saw Prince Eelin and Jaden and you here, all together. Of course." Winspur set her teacup down on the saucer so hard the tea sloshed out. "I am not surprised that Mars is at the bottom of this. Now there is a troll who would love to close the Way forever. Mars and Rud. Two of the same kind. I believe Rud himself possessed the Saqa book and destroyed it."

Annah said in an important tone, "Rud would have needed the book to create the passageway. Maybe he still has it..."

"The book is not vital... one doesn't need the book if one has the proper, er, ingredients," Winspur said. She leaned toward Annah and whispered, "The opening of the Way is one of the wisdoms passed down in the Royal family. Rud knew about the passageway from his father. When Eelin became king, Rud would tell him. But first Rud would test his son to see if he would use the wisdom in the destruction of humankind. To create a new Way and kill the human—with the last crystal, it would be finished." She shook her head. "What use is the wisdom? This is a terrible time to be human, and a terrible time to be troll. I am ashamed to say I am troll."

Annah put her hand to her head. "Terrible."

"Mars cannot take the chair. He would have me and all who think like me killed. He would have all books destroyed." Winspur looked at Annah pleadingly.

"Mars is wicked."

"That, and he is afraid. He fears knowledge and change. He fears his subjects will want to know what humans know. He's much worse than his father. Mars will find a way to rule, I have always known this. Once the father is dead. And then he will enslave the Iterians..." Winspur had a faraway look in her eyes. "You are lucky it was Eelin who found you. He is wise to hide you in Iteria where a thousand trolls live."

Annah had a thought. "When Eelin is king, he can have Mars imprisoned."

Winspur snorted. "When Eelin is king? Ha! What do you think Rud will do to Eelin when he finds out you are still alive? Eelin has disobeyed his father. I wonder if Rud knows yet?" She stroked her long hair. "Eelin cannot ever return to Haza," she said sadly. "I fear a great war."

"All because of me," Annah said.

"I never thought he would disobey his father to save a human. He must care for you a great deal, Annah." She paused and smiled. "Now don't worry, girl, the Prince has created his own problems.

"And now," Winspur said, clapping her wrinkled hands together, "enough of these despairing thoughts. Let's have a story." She leaned back in her chair. "Please tell me about your adventures, Annah, dear."

"My adventures?" she asked slowly.

"Don't be modest, now. I'm sure you've had many adventures, such as the tornado that ravaged the city, the tiger that escaped from the zoo. And you must know a story or two about a kidnapping."

Annah smiled. "I'm afraid I've never seen a tiger or a tornado, and I've especially never seen a kidnapping." She sighed. "And I've never seen a zoo, either." She began to feel sad that she had spent her entire life behind the walls of Seton House, deprived of simple things most people take for granted.

"No?" Winspur's face fell.

Annah searched her thoughts for something she might find interesting. "I can tell you about snowflakes on the window. I can tell you about winter."

"I love stories about the weather! Oh, do tell," Winspur said gleefully.

"Well, I live in a part of the world, the United States, in what's called the Midwest. There, the snow comes around December the first usually. That's the twelfth month," she explained. "It's one of the winter months. Then more snow falls, and lasts all through the winter."

"Yes, winter," Winspur repeated, closing her eyes.

"But it's very beautiful when the snow comes, especially when the sun is out. The ground is white, nothing is left uncovered, everything is the color of your hair, actually," Annah said.

"Imagine," Winspur breathed. "All white, as far as the eye can see."

Annah told her about the drifts that climb windows, and then she told about the midnight sleigh ride to town. She told about the time she tobogganed and crashed into a tree. She told her about snowmen and icepops and hot cocoa by a roaring fire. She did not tell Winspur that these events took place only once in her life, and were the result of a donation by the Church of the Honorable. She closed her eyes, and made up a story about a snow covered village at the top of the world where candy canes grow in the ground like flowers, and where her own home is as cozy and comforting as any. "I wish I could go there now," she murmured.

When Annah was finished with her story, she noticed Winspur was sitting still as a statue. Annah thought she had fallen asleep.

At last Winspur opened her eyes. "That was wonderful, child. You are a gifted storyteller."

"Thank you," Annah said. "I've a lot of experience reading stories to the children at the orphan—school."

Winspur raised an eyebrow. "Would you mind reading to me?"

Before Annah could answer Winspur went to the bookshelf. She ran a trembling hand along the tops of the books in the fiction section. "Let's see, let's see," she said happily. "Yes, this one." She took out a book and gave it to Annah. "Would you read from Colone, please? He's my favorite poet."

"Of course," Annah said. She opened to the first page of the book, where the words were written in the most beautiful gold script she had ever seen, and the pages were bordered in blue flowers. "The Primroses of Alster," she began.

"Meadow's blanket fairest yellow
Casts its color on the sky
Shadows painted on the hill
As faeries dancing floated by…"

"That was the most beautiful reading of the primroses I have ever heard," Winspur said, blotting tears from her eyes with the sleeve of her robe. "What a…" she didn't finish, for her voice was lost.

Annah blushed.

"I do wish you didn't have to go," Winspur said. "I wish you could live here instead of in Iteria. Though I understand." She smiled. "Psmet," she said.

"Psmet?" Annah repeated.

"It means 'when our paths cross' in the ancient tongue."

"I'll come back, I promise," Annah said, patting her hand.

"Greetings," a quiet voice said.

Annah turned to see Eelin and Jaden standing at the door.

"Are you ready, Annah?" Eelin asked, breathless.

"But I thought we would stay here and—and talk!" Annah said dejectedly, rising from her chair.

"I'm afraid that would not be possible," Eelin said. "I would like to stay, I wish we could."

"We have seen three Duots." Jaden touched the hilt of his sword.

Winspur rose. "You mustn't waste another moment, then."

They shook hands, Winspur touched Annah's face, and said, "When you return, we can discuss the Primroses further. And the weather." She bowed to Eelin. "Safe journey, my Lord."

Eelin patted the old troll's shoulder. "Be safe, Chronicler."

When they had left, Annah said, "What a dear old troll."

Eelin tugged hard on Salt's strap as he led her along the narrow path to the edge of the village. She was piled high with packages. "Winspur has known many humans in her life."

"I know. I have so much to tell you about my visit. About what I found out. I read Winspur a poem about primroses," Annah said. "You'd have thought I'd given her a golden watch." She wondered if Eelin knew what a watch was.

"Oh, she loves books," Eelin said. "It's a pity she cannot read them."

"What?" Annah cried. "She told me she knows how to read!"

Eelin smiled. "I'm sure she does, or did once. But the poor old troll is blind as a stone."

· FOURTEEN ·

"Blind?" Annah cried. "But that's impossible! She went to the bookshelves and picked out a book. She knew exactly where it was. She made tea and didn't spill a drop—"

"She doesn't need eyes to see," Eelin said. "She has the magic." He pulled Annah's hood close to her face just before a troop of trolls passed by headed for Sagpine. He brought his own cloak tight and nodded politely to the trolls. After they had gone he whispered, "It is said Winspur once ventured through a passageway."

"And lost her sight," Jaden finished.

"How brave of her," Annah said. "She must have really wanted to see the human world." She trudged up the steep path. The way had become mountain before she'd even realized it. Her feet had grown heavy. "But how did she know I was human?" she asked.

Eelin smiled. "Perhaps she heard your thoughts as you passed by her dwelling."

"I may have whispered," Annah said. "I may have."

"The Chronicler is a wise old one," Eelin said. And I cannot wait to hear what you have learned from her. About the Saqa." He added, in a tired voice, "Just one rotation longer, now. I too am tired." He took her arm through his. "So tired."

Annah smiled. She liked knowing that Eelin needed her strength now, that he depended on her.

Jaden muttered something to Eelin about heading northwest as opposed to northeast. Annah yawned and fought to stay awake and strong. They were in the middle of the hills of Barden and the steep climb had sucked the strength out of her.

Sometime later they arrived at their destination, a low, wide pure white rock surrounded by brown gnarled trees whose roots climbed halfway up the sides of the rock.

Annah stood blinking at the rock. "So this is..." she began, and was silenced by Eelin.

Jaden and Eelin moved the rock aside to reveal a large tunnel that descended into the darkness.

Annah peered inside. "We're going down there?"

"Just be glad you're not a mule," Jaden said jokingly. He looked up. "Dust storm coming, we arrived just in time." He led the way down the steep dirt ramp into which crude stairs had been dug. Annah followed.

Eelin whispered, "Come, Salt. You're surefooted, aren't you, mule?" He struggled as he coaxed the animal down into the tunnel.

Jaden took Annah's arm and guided her down the stairs. "You'll be able to see soon," he said.

They reached the bottom, and at first the air was musty-smelling, as though no one had disturbed the place in years, but as they went from room to room the odor of simmering herbs and broth filled the cave. Annah heard voices.

Jaden led them down a low hallway, toward a shadowy light.

"Who is there?" a deep voice hissed.

Annah stopped at the voice, but Jaden urged her along. They entered a room, dimly lit, from which three dark corridors spiked outward. A single torch burned on one wall, and it smelled like dirty oil.

From one of the corridors emerged an old male troll wearing black animal skins. He was scarred and thick, with enormous hands that gripped a dagger. He staggered forward, limping, and short of breath.

Eelin removed his cloak and helped Annah with hers. "You won't be needing this here," he said.

Jaden rushed to the old troll and they embraced. "Thank you, friend, for harboring us weary travelers this rotation," he said, laughing loudly as the elder troll sheathed his weapon.

The old troll touched Jaden's wound and said some quiet words that Annah could not understand. Then he turned to Annah, smiling with broken teeth. "I am Modoc," he told her. He bowed to Eelin. "Greetings, my Lord."

"I'm Annah," she said with a nod.

Eelin laid the cloaks across Salt's back. "Shall I stable her there?" he asked, pointing down one of the corridors.

"I'll help you," Jaden told Eelin.

They left, and Modoc said to Annah, "You'll be wanting food. Please come with me." He turned down the corridor from which he had come, and Annah followed. Who is this person? Annah wondered.

They reached a vaulted room with a long stone table and many chairs. Annah thought at first it looked like a meeting room, but it was a war room, for on the walls hung woven tapestries of trolls fighting in battle, and weapons of every sort. The swords and daggers were polished to a high sheen.

Just then a female troll entered the room along with Eelin and Jaden. She wore a sarong made of yellow leather. She was built sturdy like Modoc. "I am Graley," she said. "Welcome."

Annah introduced herself and Graley said, "It has been many a season since a human stood here." She consulted quietly with Modoc for a moment before leaving the room.

"Sit," Modoc said, taking a chair. "My wife and I have food and sleeping rooms. I am sure you are all weary."

Annah took a seat at the stone table, facing Modoc. The chairs were made of iron, with wide curved arm rests.

"Forgive my stare, but it is good to see a human," Modoc told Annah in a voice full of awe. He turned to Eelin, who had slid into the chair next to Annah. "My Lord, where is the stone?" he said in a serious tone. His nose was fat and hairs stuck out from his nostrils; his face was round as a plate and red, and when he spoke he was breathless.

Eelin sighed. "With Mars, to be sure."

Modoc spit into his hands and rubbed them together. "It is time to gather the Army of Iron."

Jaden, sitting next to Modoc, shook his head. "As long as Rud is alive, it would be difficult, if not foolish." His words came out faltering, like a question.

Graley returned with a tray piled high with food. There was broth, and smoked fish and thick bread rolled up with greenish vegetables peeking out. Graley set the food in front of Eelin and Annah, and took a chair next to Modoc. She had a pleasant, round face like her husband, and a reddish flat nose. Her eyes were pinched and black and her gray hair stuck out, and around her neck she wore a necklace of black beads. They resembled miniature cannon balls, and in the middle of each was pressed a ruby. Annah could not take her eyes from the beads; they were beautiful in a rough way.

The broth smelled like pine, though Annah doubted it was pine for there were no pine trees that she had seen. "Tila, good for the digestion," Modoc said, rubbing his stomach. He served his wife and then the others, handing each a bowl and an ornate silver spoon.

Eelin stared into his broth. "I wonder what my father is thinking this very moment," he said wistfully.

Jaden shook his head. "Probably thinking about having your teeth."

"You are not going back there!" Modoc said.

Eelin looked up. "I have to return sometime," he said. "After all, I am heir."

"I remain the Captain of your Army—and your humble servant," Modoc said with a deep nod. "And I do not advise it!" He smacked the table with his plump hands.

"Thank you, Uncle," Eelin replied.

Annah felt her face mold into a perplexed look.

Eelin gave Annah a sideways glance. He gestured with his bowl at Modoc and then at Jaden. "Father and Son," he said. "Jaden and I are cousins." He paused. "More like brothers, really."

"Father and Son," Annah repeated. She looked at Modoc. "Are you..."

"Rud's brother, yes."

Annah searched Modoc's face, trying to imagine what Rud must be like, whether he is like Modoc or different. Modoc looked more troll-like than Eelin, although she had to admit Eelin was younger and she was used to him and his quieter ways.

"My brother and I do not agree on most issues," Modoc said, as though reading Annah's mind. "Especially on the issue of humans. Which is why I live here and he lives in the Hall."

Eelin said with a sigh, "Why must brothers hate each other?"

"It seems trolls are fighting over us," Annah said. Everyone looked at her and their mouths opened as if to say something. Annah went on, "Us humans. Do you think I'm the only one?" She bit into a length of smoked fish.

All eyes went to Modoc. "Hard to say," he said. "But likely, yes. I do not know about Iteria. If any humans have walked in Iteria, who knows how many seasons ago? Before my age of wisdom, to be sure. My spies tell me nothing, but Fally would know, and perhaps Winspur."

"A human will soon walk in Iteria," Jaden said, grinning. "Unless the Duots have us for soup first."

Annah leaned her head on her hand, and watched as the trolls continued to talk about the situation. After a while she began to nod. She had never been so tired.

Modoc stood suddenly and announced, "We will prepare the rooms now! And the travelers will sleep."

Graley took Annah's arm and led her down the hallway. "There is a place to wash just there," she told her, pointing to an airy room of white granite where an iron tub stood all by itself. "I've set out nightclothes, and if you leave your garments outside the room I will have them clean by the waking rotation."

Graley poured Annah a bath from water that she brought in a large bowl. She brought bowl after bowl until the tub was full, and would not let Annah help. Then she brought hot stones which she set into notches in the sides of the tub. She placed an iron partition at the door to guard the entrance.

Annah washed her body and hair with a lemony ball of soap. She dried herself and donned her nightclothes, a billowy sack of rough brown fabric.

Graley led Annah to her room, and eased her into the softest cot Annah could imagine. The room smelled faintly of lemons. The moment Annah sank into bed she fell into the deep sea of her dreams.

ಲ೦೮

A soft hand stroked her forehead.
"Annah, dear, wake up, it's time for breakfast."
Annah opened her eyes to see the sun streaming into the room. The walls and ceiling were covered in paper of pale blue bachelor buttons and goldenrod. Everywhere she looked she saw the blue and yellow flowers, which made her feel like she was enveloped in a sunny garden. The room seemed to close in on her, but it was not an unpleasant feeling.
A woman was bent over her. She smelled of anise and her face was kind. Her hair was dark red and long and it curled softly toward her face, and the eyes were pale blue violet.
"Did you sleep well?"
"Yes, Mother," Annah replied.

ಲ೦೮

Annah blinked and looked around the dim room. She inhaled, but the air was thick with smoke, and it made her cough. The blue and yellow flowers were gone. The sunlight had disappeared. "How did things change so quickly?" she murmured, still half-asleep.

She stumbled out of the cot and made her way down the hall, following the light. "Mother," she murmured, realizing that of course she had been dreaming about Mrs. Atherton, the woman from the orphanage, and that she was in a cave and not in a sunny bedroom.

Annah padded into the room where they had met the night before. The eating-table had been cleared.

Eelin sat in the same chair, his head resting on folded arms. On the table in front of him lay his sword in its scabbard. His waist-length braids were tied back with a leather strap that was knotted with several large knots. He wore a clean white shirt with puffy sleeves.

As Annah approached, Eelin sat up and rubbed his eyes.

"Annah, come here," he whispered, gesturing with his chin.

"Have you slept in the chair all this time?"

Eelin blinked. "In the chair, yes. But I have not slept much."

Annah wondered how long she herself had slept. She felt rested, so she supposed she had been asleep for many hours. In another room she heard snoring. She sat down next to Eelin, and brushed her long curls away from her eyes.

"Did you sleep well?" Eelin asked.

"Yes," Annah answered with a start. *'Did you sleep well?'* Her mother's words in the dream. Already the dream was a fading memory. But the memory was being replaced by the realization that Eelin cared for her. It occurred to her that she was safe here with Eelin, as safe as with her mother in the dream. I wonder if the dream about my mother is really a dream about Eelin, she wondered, then brushed the idea aside. "How much longer to Iteria?" she asked.

Eelin furrowed his brow. "Perhaps nine or ten rotations."

Roughly twenty hours, Annah thought, surprised at her ability to translate the time, as though time were a foreign language. "Do you think we'll make it safely?"

Eelin smiled, but his eyes were sad. "If there is any justice, we will make it."

"And what will happen after we get to Iteria?"

"I suppose you will stay with Mave until I…"

"Until you find the stone?"

"Until I find the stone," he repeated without emotion.

"And afterward?" Annah asked. "Will you come back to Iteria?"

Eelin looked at the torch glowing on the opposite wall and his eyes seemed to absorb the fire. "In the name of Roex, I will come back."

"To unite the kingdoms," Annah said.

Eelin laughed bitterly. He didn't look at her. "If my brother has his way, I will watch him rule from my prison cell."

Without thinking, Annah gripped his arm, and fought the urge to reach out and touch his shiny hair. "We could fight Mars. The Army of

Iron. The Army and the Iterians together. There are more Iterians than Hazans, right?" Her voice was high and excited. I never thought I'd be talking about war, she thought. I never thought I'd ever see an army, much less be part of one. I thought I'd be a teacher all my life. A nice, ordinary life.

"I'm afraid it must come to war," Eelin said quietly, stroking the hilt of the sword. He looked strangely pale, Annah thought. Perhaps it was the torch light.

Annah cleared her throat. "I never noticed the design on the handle of your sword, of your blade, before," she said. She leaned closer and looked at the flattish silver symbol surrounded by a pewter colored metal. "It's a sunburst, isn't it?"

"Yes. But it is not my blade." He unsheathed the sword and pushed it across the table to her.

She looked at her reflection in the center of the sun, and on the gleaming blade as she carefully ran her hand along the edge. Then her eyes went to the wall to see where the sword had come from. She looked in the reflection again, and drew back in surprise. Her hands went to her face, her hair. The face in the reflection was a stranger. Her face had thinned, and her eyes had deepened into their sockets. "I look old," she murmured. And then she asked herself, not the usual, am I pretty? But rather, am I brave enough? She thought, I'm so far away from the girl I was at Seton House. So alone. And yet—and yet, I feel like I'm home.

"What is the sword made of?" she asked finally. It was more brilliant than the shiniest silver, and looked sharper than a razor.

"Nicon," he replied. "Nickel, steel, and carbon. Not as fine as what can be bought in Atold, but still it is a good enough blade. Pick it up. I had the sunburst fixed to it at the last moment—" his voice broke.

She hoisted up the sword with two hands and began to wield it at an imaginary Duot. "It's so heavy," she groaned. "How can you stand it?"

"You will get used to it," Eelin said, looking solemnly into her eyes.

Annah stopped the sword in midair. "Is this..."

"Yes. The blade is for you." He reached into his pocket and took out a sharpening stone and set it in front of her. Then he took her hands in his and brought her hands close to his face. He kissed the blade softly and said, "May you fight well."

· FIFTEEN ·

Annah carefully set the blade, <u>her</u> blade, on the stone table. If only Headmistress Downing could see me now, she thought, using the sleeve of her nightgown to clean the fingerprints from the sharp surface. What would Miss Downing think of Haza, and of Eelin and Jaden? She tried to conjure up Miss Downing's face aghast, but all she could see was a gray braid at the nape of a thin neck. It was all she could remember of the face she had seen every day for most of her fourteen years.

    I don't need to go back to Seton quite yet, Annah thought casually. I have things to do here first. She picked up the blade in her right hand. It felt a little lighter than it did a moment ago, and strangely comfortable, as though it was designed to fit her, as though she had used it before. She set it down again.

"Jaden and I purchased the blade in Sagpine while you were visiting the Chronicler," Eelin was saying. "Do you like it?"

Annah said, "I like it. But I don't know how to use it."

"That is easily remedied," a voice called from across the room.

Annah turned around to see Jaden standing in the corridor rubbing his head. "It's a good blade, isn't it?" He sauntered over to the table.

"Yes," Annah replied.

"May you slay many a Duot and fight tyranny for all time," Jaden said reverently.

"Will you show me how to wield the sword?" She directed her question to both of them.

Eelin bowed his head to Jaden. "He is the master of the blade."

"Nonsense, cousin," Jaden said.

"Did you not save my life three times?"

Before Jaden could answer Modoc entered bearing a tray of food and steaming drink. "I trust all slept well?" he boomed.

"We're fit to fight," Jaden answered with determination.

Modoc set the tray down slowly. "May you encounter no one to fight."

After the meal they prepared to leave. Standing assembled in the room, they stared at one another, no one wanting to start the good-byes. Above ground, Salt had been tethered to a brittle stalagmite and was packed with fresh provisions.

Finally Eelin clasped arms with Modoc. "Be well, uncle."

"And you, my Lord," Modoc replied. "Send word when you reach Iteria."

Modoc and Graley hugged and kissed Jaden. "Safe return, son," they said.

Graley vanished down one of the corridors. She returned with an arm behind her back, smiling mischievously. She shuffled up to Annah and handed her a wide leather belt decorated with iron beads like the ones she wore at her neck. Each bead held a ruby in its center.

Graley laughed, her eyes small and dark like the beads.

"It's beautiful," Annah said. The belt was well-worn, and powdery soft, yet heavy as it was thickly turned.

"I'm too old for this now," Graley said. "Though I'm keeping my sword. Just in case." She winked.

"Graley has slain a Duot," Modoc said.

"In my dreams I have slain many more than that," Graley added.

Annah felt her mouth twitch into a smile.

"Where do you think Jaden learned his swing of the sword?" Modoc went on.

"Oh, stop, husband." Graley nudged Modoc's fat gut with her elbow. She turned to Annah. "Good luck, girl."

Annah bowed to them when she said good-bye.

೫○೫

Soon they would be able to see Iteria, Eelin told Annah as they made their way along the path. They would know they were close when they saw two white boulders in the shape of columns, the symbol of peace. But this last hill of Barden was fiercely high, it was more mountain than hill, and Annah doubted she could make it to Iteria without sleep. It had been many rotations since they had left Modoc's—eleven, Eelin had counted, not the nine or ten he had estimated earlier. They were all exhausted, even Salt, whose breath heaved with every step.

Annah had insisted on wearing her sword, which only made sense, she thought. But the cloak was hot, and the weight of the sword all that way uphill had worn her out before they had gone far from the underground cavern. She had doubts about whether she could even get the sword out of its scabbard should she need to.

"Let us rest briefly, I am tired," Eelin said.

They all stopped. "Thank you," Annah said, glancing sideways at him, wondering if he had stopped for her benefit. She watched as he gazed toward the mountain crowned with black trees. After a short while he said, "Annah, are you ready to go on?"

She managed a weak smile. "Yes, but this sword is going to take some getting used to, I'm afraid. It's awfully heavy."

Several times while climbing the steep mountain she held tight to the hilt of the sword and it seemed to give her a second wind. When they stopped to rest Jaden thrust his blade at her and she dodged it quicker than she had expected. She drew her sword, jabbed at Jaden's chest, and he skidded back. They touched blades, circling each other. The blades went up, points touching. Annah's two hands gripped the sword hilt, Jaden's left hand held his sword firmly.

"Let us cross blades without touching, see if you can do it," Jaden said. "I do not want to hear a sound."

Annah began to spar with him in silence. She moved her blade slowly and silently, following the movements of Jaden's blade. When he moved quicker, she followed. Then she dropped the blade in the dirt. "I'll never learn this. My wrist will break before I learn."

"Practice," he told her.

Annah knew Jaden took the business of sword fighting seriously. It was the only thing he took seriously.

As they neared the summit of the mountain, darkness fell upon Annah like a blanket, and her eyes began to feel prickly, and heavy, as though something were pressing on them. She rubbed her eyes and the mountain top came into focus. What's more, she could make out the finer facial details of Jaden and Eelin, as though they had been hidden from her all this time and were now being illuminated by a candle that burned above their heads.

"I wonder," she said "if my eyes are becoming accustomed to the dark." She turned to Eelin, wide-eyed. "How much light is there at this spot?"

"What do you mean?"

"Are we in total darkness?"

Eelin furrowed his black brow. "It would appear that there is very little light in this region. What do you think, Jaden?"

"I never thought of it before, but I suppose there is only the stalactite glow reflecting off the cavern top," he said, looking up. "Other than that I perceive nothing."

Annah too looked up. The roof of the cavern, which seemed as far away as rain clouds back home, glowed a greenish yellow with crystallized bumps. "I think my eyes are becoming used to your world," she told Eelin.

Her blindness was replaced with energy and strength. Her ability to see took away the last remnants of fear, like the night light at Seton House that eased her into sleep when she had awoken from a bad dream.

Before long they stood on the mountain top and Iteria lay sprawled below, heavily forested, dotted with quartz caves and in the far distance, tall structures and a ribbon of red.

"I can't believe we've made it," she said brightly. She looked at the two tall stones at the bottom of the steep mountainside.

Jaden and Eelin gazed around suspiciously.

"It is most quiet," Eelin said, touching his sword hilt.

"We have only a short measure to go, cousin." Jaden's smile was tight and cautious.

They made their way halfway down the winding road into Iteria. The topography had been changing since they left Modoc's, but now on this side of the mountain odd tree formations had sprouted. Annah thought their texture was like mud heaps. The ground had grown slippery and green.

"Are they trees?" Annah whispered. "Is it really a forest?"

Beside her, Eelin nodded yes, then no.

Annah touched a tree as she passed it. It felt like a soaked sponge.

Annah looked down to the base of the mountain where dense bramble grew and just beyond that stood the tall white boulders jutting out of the ground like two elephant tusks.

"The stones," Jaden whispered, nodding with his chin.

They stood looking, breathless. Jaden fed Salt seeds from the pack, spilling half of them on the ground.

Annah couldn't wait to meet Mave, and wondered if they were near the same age, and whether they had anything in common. Would we become friends? I wonder if she has human qualities like Eelin? We could be like sisters. The thought gave her a burst of energy, and she picked up her step, stretching ahead of the others, trying to keep from sliding down the wet hill by digging in with her boot heels.

She pulled her cloak around her as a chilling breeze blew across her face. It was as though someone had just brushed past her, like the flutter of a bird's wing. And there was an odd smell. Perhaps it was just the forges far away.

There came an odd rasping noise. She spun around to see Eelin clutching at his neck. His face was twisted into a terrible scream, but no sound came out except for gasps. His eyes bulged. Salt stood a few paces off, and Jaden, with his back to Annah, was still feeding her.

"Eelin, what is it?" Annah asked, scrambling up to him. He was choking, tearing at his neck with one hand, but waving her away with the other hand. She held her breath as a sound rang in her ears, Eelin's cry of panic and pain. There came a word in a tongue she did not know, a growling, guttural language. She dared not get any closer to Eelin. He had been caught in a stranglehold by an unseen Duot.

Jaden rushed to Eelin's side, only to be sent flying to the ground.

Annah watched in horror as Eelin was dragged toward the thick mat of trees. An invisible death had come upon them, and she was powerless to stop it.

"Run, Annah," Eelin whispered in a voice that sounded like a claw dragged across a stone.

Annah's hand went to her sword but she could not seem to get it unsheathed. At the same moment, something from behind caught her arm with a grip like iron tongs. She cried out in anger and frustration. At last she pulled the sword from its scabbard, and it flashed silver in the air. She wrenched herself halfway around and plunged the blade her with all her might, and felt the sword ripping into flesh, and scraping bone. Annah twisted the blade free. Dark blood ran down the hilt, down her arm, dripped off her elbow.

The Duot she had stabbed came into focus on the ground, bathed in a pool of blood from a gaping wound to its chest. Although it was dead or near death, hate still blazed in its agate eyes. Annah whipped around. Eelin was nowhere to be seen. A few paces off, Jaden lay face down in the dirt, motionless. Blood trickled from a deep slice above his right ear.

"No!" she cried. So much had happened in just a few moments' time. She glanced around crazily, looking for help, wondering what to do. But there was nobody to help. She was alone. She wiped her blade across the Duot's leather vest, drew a deep breath and tightened her grip on the hilt. For the first time, she felt the earth below her shudder at a geyser's marking of rotation.

Annah focused all of her energy and thought, I need *help*.

She turned and ran downhill, blind instinct fueled by terror, toward the white boulders. She tumbled down the deep descents of the hill, through the wet, rotting trees, wrestled through a bramble wall, and crossed into Iteria.

PART II

· SIXTEEN ·

Annah did not stop running when she reached the white boulders. She did not pause to look back. What good would it do? The Duots with their magic could, at any moment, be right behind her, snatching at her with deadly talons. She had to keep going, though her legs were numb and shaking. Her lungs burned as though there were embers inside them. What a cruel joke that they were overtaken by Duots with Iteria so close. Mars planned it that way, Annah was sure of it.

She kept running, never stopping, until every breath came as a wheezing cough. She descended through deep layers of rotting things, ever-thickening and hanging with greenish muck. In some places the muck rose well past her knees; it was like wading through a pool of sludge.

The sword in her swollen hand was dragging through the mud now, as was the scabbard that hung on the iron-studded belt. "What good is this stupid sword?" she asked herself. "I should not have left Jaden." She cried miserably, letting the tears soak her cheeks and pour down the bridge of her nose. "He might have been alive. I could have helped him."

She could not bear to even think about Eelin, afraid that doing so would assure his death. "If I don't mention his name he will be all right," she whispered.

Yet thoughts of him bombarded her. Guilt overcame her as she remembered back to their first encounter when she fell through the passageway. She had hated him, thought him hideously ugly. Now she tried to undo the bad thoughts, as though it would bring him back to life. She remembered the first moment her eyes saw him, tried to bring him into clear focus, and tried to see him in a new way. She concentrated on his goodness, and on his face that was open and kind. Though she could not summon up the exact color of brown of his eyes, she could feel their depth and honesty.

A pang of hopelessness crushed her. She had deserted him—after he had spared her life—and she had deserted Jaden, too, and even Salt: she had left the poor creature to starve to death.

"I am a coward," she muttered. She stopped and turned to look at the mountain she had just come down. She thought about climbing back up through the muck. Eelin had told her to run, and she had run. But to what end? She was alive, but alone. The thought crossed her mind that she should return to bury Jaden's body.

She slowed her pace and looked around at this vast, awful mudbath called Iteria. In addition to forests, it was cluttered with boulders large and small. "Nothing but rocks," she said, wiping her tears on the heavy cloak still wet with the Duot's blood. "A wasteland."

Iteria was not the beautiful place she had imagined. "I'm going back," she told herself. "To bury Jaden."

Behind her a step sounded and she whipped around. Her scabbard dug a circle in the mud and came to rest in front of her, and she withdrew her sword and held it out with trembling hands. "Show yourself, Duot!" she cried.

A form emerged from behind a tree.

"Salt!" She ran to the mule and threw her arms around the beast's neck and nuzzled the warm fur, smelling its odor of dirt and seed. "I'm so glad you're all right. If only Jaden and Eelin..."

"Jaden made it," a weak voice said, and she looked up to see Jaden stumbling toward her.

"Oh, you're alive!" Annah cried, rushing to hug him.

"It would seem so." He held his hand to his ear and Annah saw dark blood ooze between his fingers. "I have not kept my promise very well, have I?"

Annah could not look at his face without tears starting in her eyes. You're not supposed to look so sad, she wanted to tell him. "What promise?"

"To see that you and Eelin arrive safely in Iteria."

"You're wounded," she said, changing the subject. She took his head in her hands to examine the bloody spot.

"It's just a scrape," he muttered. "Though a painful scrape, I must admit."

"It's all my fault. If not for me the Duots wouldn't have…"

"No, girl," Jaden said, touching her arm. "It was Eelin they wanted."

"Do you think he's dead?" she forced herself to ask. She held the cleanest part of her cloak to the gash below his ear to stop the bleeding.

"Worse than that, I suspect," Jaden said, his face folding into bitter sadness. "Worse than that."

Annah felt a desperate need to open Salt's pack, take out Abbi and hug her. Instead she clutched the hilt of her sword. "I don't believe he's dead. Come on," she said. "Let's find Mave. She'll know what to do. She can help us rescue him."

Jaden snickered. "You do not know her," he said. "She is the last person who can help."

Annah ignored his comments, and wiped the dirt and tears from her face. She removed the cloak she had been wearing, hiding behind, and wrapped it around Jaden's neck like a muffler bandage. "Then I'll do it myself," she said. She sheathed her sword, took Salt's lead in her hand, pointed herself toward the valley and began to walk.

Jaden caught up with her. "We'll do it together," he said. "Fally might be able to help us."

"The wizard, of course!" Annah said, remembering what Jaden had said before.

They trudged ahead. The trees thickened and grew blacker, wet and dense with a pungent, ammonia smell. Annah touched the trunk of one of the trees as she passed by. It was slimy, like a slug. The air, too, was wet and made her skin feel slippery, as though the sky were raining oil.

"What kind of trees are these?" Annah asked. She looked up into the umbrella-shaped branches. Before Jaden could answer she realized what it was. "Mushroom," she murmured. "A huge mushroom."

She turned to Jaden. "Is it edible?"

"Yes," he answered. "Mostly. As long as it is black. Never touch a white one, or it's instant death."

"Where I come from mushrooms are the size of your thumb."

Jaden shook his head. "What a strange world, yours."

"What a strange world yours," she repeated without emotion.

The air stayed wet as they walked along, and finally Jaden returned Annah's bloodied cloak, draping it over her arm. "I'm all right now," he said.

"I think it's raining."

"Welcome to Iteria," Jaden said. He turned left at a fork in the road they had come to, as the brown rain fell, soaking them. It oozed from the mat of trees overhead.

"Iteria is a mushroom rain forest," Annah said, wiping the pungent liquid from her cheeks.

"The ground is particularly rich and porous. And if you listen carefully you can hear the waterfalls," Jaden said.

Before long the rain stopped, the forest thinned and they stood in a huge clearing. The land had become, without Annah realizing it, a desert of white clay and rocks. As they walked, with each step, bone-dry puffs of clay rose up like clouds. The rocks were magnetic, and their swords tilted toward them when they walked by. The beginnings of a stream had started too, just a trickle near their feet. It was blood red, the stripe Annah had seen from the mountain top.

"The stream will lead to the city and Mave's cavern," Jaden said. "Her palace, I mean."

They stopped to rest only once, and continued down into the valley, following the stream, which, by the time they had reached the center of the city, had become a wide river. Annah could see troll children playing by the bank, dunking one another. The river ran along a shallow bed of white oval stones that looked like huge prehistoric eggs.

They walked along the river bank, and the children and Annah exchanged glances. Annah had never seen so many children. Judging by their stares they had never seen the likes of Annah. Many of them smiled in a shy way and watched Annah with huge, curious eyes. One of them touched her cloak and giggled as she passed by. There were adults, too, sitting together in small groups. Strange that they aren't watching their children, Annah thought.

"They like you," Jaden said.

They traced the river a little farther and crossed a stone bridge. "Come on Salt," Jaden told the beast. "Just a little farther." But she stopped in the middle of the bridge and would not move until she was fed.

Soon they came to a tall, ivory stone structure that to Annah resembled a castle with turrets. It was almost completely oval and around the oval windows red glass had been pressed. "It's lovely," she said. She managed a smile. "I'm glad we're here at last."

Jaden snorted and said, "We'll see," as he tied Salt to an iron post outside the palace door, and then he led Annah through the unlocked door to a marble-floored hall. Down the smooth arched corridor they went, passing trolls who stared at Annah.

Jaden smiled and said, "Good health," and "peace to you," showing the palms of his hands.

At last they reached a set of circular stairs which they climbed. At the top of the stairs stood a huge iron door. Jaden lifted the silver knocker and let it fall.

A young female servant opened the door, bowing. She disappeared and soon an old male troll came to the doorway. Annah thought his eyes were the same pale, colorless eyes as Winspur's, but they didn't have the same vacant quality to them. They were keen as they studied first Jaden and then Annah. He looked at her like he could not get enough of her, the way one would stare at a huge, dazzling diamond.

Annah studied him as well. He was rather tall for a troll, and bone thin. He was completely bald, but along his ears gray hair grew in long tufts. His teeth were sharp, though all the lowers were missing. His tongue kept rolling out and licking his lower lips as though looking for the lost teeth.

He seemed to recognize Jaden at last, and his eyes blinked wildly. "Jaden! What a surprise," he said. "Mave will be so pleased. Please do come in, both of you. I am Fally." He took Annah's hand and shook it, his hand frail as paper in hers.

"My name is Annah," she told him.

They stepped into a beautiful round room lined with glass tables. On the tables stood glass ornaments and bowls. Most of the glass was pink in color and simple in design. Paintings hung on the walls—well-crafted pictures of troll families and odd flowers and birds.

One side of the room had an enormous window, and the view seemed to go on forever, Annah thought.

In front of the window stood a slender figure in an ivory fur robe. It was Mave, Annah figured, and she did not seem to notice them, for her back was to them and she seemed to be studying something in the distance.

"Company, Mave," Fally announced giddily, drawing Annah close.

Mave turned slowly and padded over to them. She did not look anything like what Annah had pictured. In fact, she could barely pass for a troll. She had a smallish nose, luxurious brown hair that hung well past her shoulders, and her eyes were golden and shaped like a cat's. There was no hair on her face, and her cheekbones were high and flat. Around her neck she wore a necklace of brilliant emeralds, each the size of a hen's egg.

"Mave, it's good to see you," Jaden said wryly.

Mave sniffed at him in a dismissive way. She glided over to Annah, stared at her from her head to toe, tilted her head this way and that. "*Who* and *what* are you?" she demanded.

· SEVENTEEN ·

"Grandfather, who is this?" Mave asked, as though Annah were not in the room.

"Why don't you ask me yourself, I do speak," Annah said, surprised at how rude her answer came out. She was beginning to feel the insignificance of it all—the splendor of the castle, the beautiful princess with a flowing robe and sharp tongue. I have more important things to do than stand here, Annah thought. Just let me rest a few rotations and I'll be on my way back to Haza to look for Eelin.

"Well?" Mave went on, tapping her gold slipper on the floor.

"Mave, your manners!" Fally said. "I'm sorry, Annah," he said humbly. "You must forgive her. She has never seen a human."

At the word human Mave swayed backward as though thrown off balance. "You are a human?" she shrilled. "I thought you were a—mistake."

"She's Annah, and she is not a mistake," Jaden said indignantly. He pulled Annah away from Mave, toward a smaller eating area off to the side. "Do not let her words hurt you," he whispered.

Mave followed and reached out and touched Annah's arm. "Please," she said. "It's just that I did not expect a human to be like you." Standing before Annah, she looked into her eyes. "Hmmm. You are not that different from us, no. I expected a filthy—although you are not exactly clean—foul-smelling..."

Annah's hand went to her mouth. "Different enough, and I'm glad," she muttered into her cupped hand.

Mave seemed sorry for what she had said. "You are not frightening. You are almost pleasing, yes."

Annah rolled her eyes.

Mave stroked Annah's hair. "Odd color, but interesting," she said. Her hand went to her own hair. "I wonder if rust would make my hair the same?" She smiled with small white teeth that had been filed sharp and studded with diamonds. Her face was dusted with white powder that, from a distance, hid the fine dark hairs that grew on her skin. Clipped to her ears were golden coins dotted with rubies. She looked to be a few years older than Eelin and Jaden.

Annah glanced at Jaden with his grimy face, his crooked smile, and long ears that stuck out. It was hard to believe they were of the same species.

Mave crossed into the larger room and began to regard her hair in front of a free-standing mirror. She stood with her back to the mirror, looking over her shoulder.

Fally joined Annah and Jaden in the eating area where a copper table and chairs stood, enclosed on three sides by walls of cupboards and shelves. "Sit now, and I'll prepare food and drink," he said. He wobbled away and disappeared down a corridor.

Jaden and Annah removed their belts and swords and set them on a wooden bench in an alcove near the table. They each took a chair and sat, speechless, as they watched Mave in the adjoining room primp in front of the mirror.

Annah kept reminding herself that Mave, in her own rough way, had been trying to be complimentary.

Across the table Jaden said, "She has much to learn. About everything."

"Thirsty?" Fally said. He entered the room carrying a tray of food and drink.

"Of course, grandfather," Mave said, turning to follow him. "We have company."

Fally set before them a large earthen jug, glasses, and bread with brownish jelly on it.

Mave seated herself next to her grandfather. Annah caught her staring from across the table. After a while Annah didn't care.

Jaden stared blankly at the food and drink for a long moment and then looked up and said, "Eelin has been taken."

Mave's eyes widened, but she said nothing.

On Fally's face there came a look of horror. The fruit-smelling drink he was pouring into Annah's cup sloshed onto the table and he set the jug down and blotted the liquid with a cloth.

Annah and Jaden explained all that had happened on the road, and Fally listened, murmuring and shaking his head. "I have never trusted Mars. Or Rud. But the prince, poor fellow."

"It's all her fault, you know," Mave said.

Fally silenced Mave with a slap to the wrist. He looked at Annah with tired eyes. "Nonsense, human. You have been chosen. Your story will be told in troll legend for all time."

Annah put her head in her hands. "I don't want to be chosen…"

"You may very well be the last human in all of our underground world," Fally went on.

Jaden smirked. "If Mars has his way, there won't be a living troll _or_ human in our underground world. Mars _will_ bring war to Iterian soil. I know it."

"All you ever think of is war and killing," Mave said. "I am sick of hearing about it, yes."

"Sometimes war is necessary," Annah heard herself say. She thought of the Duot she had killed with her sword and was glad. "It is necessary, but terrible," she said.

Annah watched as Jaden's eyes bore into Fally's. "We must have a plan and quickly." He shifted his gaze to a small iron object on the table and laid his hand over the spherical shape.

Annah, too, looked at the object. It was a sundial.

"From a friend in Sagpine," Fally said, smiling at Annah. He drew a deep breath. "Would Rud have the prince killed for treason?"

"I cannot fathom," Jaden said, "that Rud would kill his son who is so like his beloved Hela. But we all know that Rud is not long for this life, if he lives still. Then it will be Mars..." He paused. "And if Eelin is alive, he's in prison, and what manner of torture he is being subject to, one can only imagine. Every moment brings him closer to death. If we could take your best trolls and gather my father's army, we could be in Haza..."

Fally sat up stiffly in the chair. "I am at your service."

"We could use your magic, Sir," Jaden said. "With the Duots, we will need all the magic we can get."

"Grandfather, it is too dangerous for you!" Mave shrieked, revealing the first inkling of concern for someone besides herself.

"It is she who is in danger," Fally said, pointing at Annah.

Annah gave Jaden a pleading look. "You said I would be safe in Iteria."

"Which is exactly why you will stay here," Fally said matter-of-factly.

The plan hit Annah like a mallet. *Fally and Jaden are going back to Haza to rescue Eelin and I'm stuck here,* she thought. "I'm not staying," she said firmly. "With..." She started to say, "With Mave," but caught herself and said, "without Eelin."

"You would be killed the instant you set foot in Haza!" Fally cried. He glanced at her sword lying across the wooden bench, and his voice softened. "I see that you are brave, girl, but it would not help Eelin for you to be killed."

"So I'm to stay here by myself while you...?"

"Mave will be here," Fally said without looking at her. He stood and smoothed his white silken robe. "And she will take care of you."

"I will?" Mave asked.

Fally gave her a stern look. "Yes, you will."

Annah muttered under her breath, "I'd rather die fighting Duots."

· EIGHTEEN ·

Annah had, before sleep, raided Salt's packs and retrieved Abbi and her book, *Adventure on the High Seas.* Wrapped in the leather bag were the books from Eelin: *The Journey of King Sinclair,* and *Country Bear.* She had been surprised and delighted to see them, and wished she could have read them to Eelin before he was taken.

She had risen early, had sat on her cot, holding the books in her lap, waiting for Fally and Jaden to come and say good-bye. She kept quiet, eavesdropping on a disturbing conversation taking place in the next chamber.

Fally and Mave were arguing. It was early in the rotation, and Fally had been preparing to leave.

"You will do your queenly duties," he said to Mave.

"I don't want to," Mave retorted.

"You will protect the human," Fally said in hushed tones. "Don't you understand the seriousness of it all, granddaughter? She is the last!"

"Why don't you take her with you?" Mave whined. "Please don't leave me. I'm not a mother. Besides, she will bring bad luck."

"Mave!" Fally cried. "This is nonsense. Do you not care for your people, and for your own fate?"

"It wasn't my idea to be Queen," Mave said angrily.

"You have royal blood, you possess a soul," Fally said. "It is your duty."

"My only duty is to die," Mave said bitterly. "Like Mother and Father." She began to cry.

"It is not the girl's fault your parents died," Fally said kindly.

"Had they not made the journey to Haza they would have been spared. The humans killed them."

"Not Annah."

"Her kind brought the disease," Mave said in a cruel voice.

"The girl can teach you much."

"Oh?"

"I'm sure she can read," Fally said.

There was a long moment of silence. "I suppose," Mave said, "I would like to make poetry like that which Mother recited, yes..."

"That and more," Fally said excitedly. "You could read of magic and lore. Who knows," he laughed. "You might even find the book, where all knowledge is kept. You would know more magic than I myself know. Think of it. The power!"

Mave said, in a faraway-sounding voice, "It is hard to know words. I have tried."

"There it is, Mave. You two can help each other. The human mind's eye cannot easily see the magic. There are too absorbed in critical thought. Be glad for what you are and for what she is. Learn from each other."

"Perhaps..." Mave said. "And the human will earn her keep with me."

"There's a good girl," Fally said. "Promise you will be kind to Annah."

"All right," Mave said. "But you know the prophesy—that a human will bring civil war. War, yes."

"To be specific, a troll and human together," Fally corrected her. "Do not be so quick to blame."

The conversation ceased when Jaden entered the room wishing Mave a good life.

Annah climbed out of her cot and began to get dressed. Jaden came a short while later, and together they went downstairs to the great room.

They embraced and Jaden whispered, "Be well, and do not worry. I will bring him back."

Fally came downstairs wearing a suit of rabbit skins, and at his side a gleaming nicon and gold sword. He touched Annah's shoulder and said, "We will return soon." He lowered his voice and said, "Take care of Mave. She has no one else." Then they were gone.

Mave did not come down to say good-bye.

Annah sat at the copper table. She stared at the sundial, wishing she could turn back time.

Besides being stuck with Mave, which was worse than being stuck alone, she feared that once she let Jaden out of her sight she would lose him the way she had lost Eelin. She could not imagine herself staying here and growing to like Mave like she had envisioned earlier.

She entertained the notion of rescuing Eelin on her own, the two of them running, hiding out, and coming back to Iteria safely. "I wonder," she whispered, touching the sundial, "if I could find my way back to Haza?" There was only one road. But it was a long one.

Annah went to her chamber, took out the books Eelin had given her, and curled up in the chair next to the cot. The chair was covered in stippled leather, with a soft blanket draped over one arm. On the table next to the chair a candle in an iron claw burned, splaying leafy shadows across her book.

Perhaps if I ignore Mave, she will leave me alone, Annah thought. She opened *The Journey of King Sinclair* and began to read quietly, pretending the children at Seton House were there as her audience. "Once, when the light of morning came up huge and of a yellow never seen..."

Annah looked up to see Mave standing before her.

"You are reading that book?" Mave asked.

"What did you think I was doing with it?" Annah snapped.

Mave's mouth curled into a pout. But she regained her composure and said proudly, "I have many books."

"Do you?" Annah asked, looking around. "Where?" And what good are they if you can't read, she wanted to say.

"In the Gallery, in the City of Glass," Mave said.

"The Gallery?"

"There are more books than can be counted."

Annah felt a sense of relief, and smiled, because now there was a way for the time to pass quicker. "Will you take me to the Gallery?"

"If you wish," Mave said with a smirk.

"What kind of books do you have there?"

"All kinds, yes," Mave answered. "But most wonderful is the one of the Ancients that explain the great magic of the Saqa."

"But that book is with Rud. Isn't it?" Annah said. "It's the most—sacred. You know where the book is?"

Mave narrowed her eyes. "Not exactly, but perhaps we can find it, yes."

Annah shook her head slowly. "And what good is the book without the stone, the crystal? We'll never get that back because Mars has it."

Mave said, "I don't believe it is the last stone."

"You think there's another one somewhere?"

"How do you know there is not? Grandfather said the ancient book tells where all the stones were kept."

"He saw the book?"

"No."

"Then how does he know?"

"The Chronicler, of course."

Annah was speechless. "I don't believe it. I have met Winspur and she didn't tell me..."

Mave shrugged. "My grandfather and Winspur are of the same family. They share magic you could never understand, human."

Annah was perplexed and angry. "I know some things that your grandfather might not," she said coldly. "I know, for instance, that you could live in my world if you wanted to. Live there without dying from the sunlight."

Mave tugged at her brown hair, pulled a strand to her lips and twisted it like a mustache. "And how is this possible?"

"It's all in the book," Annah said proudly. "The same book of the Saqa."

"Do you really think I could walk in your world?" Mave asked. "Would I want to?" Her hands went to her teeth and then pointed to Annah's. "Do you think my teeth could be made to look like yours?"

Annah rolled her eyes.

"If we could find the book you could read it, and we could find another stone..." Mave's voice trailed off.

"Then let's go," Annah said, climbing out of the chair.

"But there is something, just one thing, yes," Mave said. "Finding the book in the Gallery may be like finding a crumb of dirt on a mountain."

· NINETEEN ·

"We might as well keep busy while they're gone," Annah said. "And looking for a book is a good way to keep busy." She followed Mave down the hallway. Shall I get my cloak?"

Mave laughed. "What? That hideous thing? I wouldn't be caught..." She stopped, and said in a kinder voice, "You won't need a cloak to hide behind. You are safe here. Mostly because the Iterians won't know what to think of you."

"Will we go by mule?"

"I should say not. We shall travel down the Andor." She turned on her heel. "Now come to my chamber and change out of that ragged thing."

Annah looked down at her flowered dress, torn, full of mud, and blood-stained. She had to admit the dress seemed out of place here.

They went to Mave's chamber and Mave opened a pair of wooden doors revealing a wardrobe built into the white stone wall. Annah saw rows and rows of clothes hanging on pegs. Mave withdrew a white leather dress with round rubies attached to the sleeves and hem. She handed the dress to Annah.

The garment was heavier than it looked. Annah undressed down to her camisole and pulled the dress over her head. It tied at the neck in front, and beads hung from the leather ties. She turned to face the full-length mirror that hung on the wall next to the wardrobe.

"How odd I look," she said. "We have nothing like this where I come from." The dress was loose on her bony frame and hung past her knees and flared just above the ankles. "This will take some getting used to," she said with a grin. She ran her hands along the soft leather.

"You may keep the dress," Mave said easily. "I have more, yes."

"Thank you." Annah pulled her red hair into a bun on top of her head and held it there a moment before she let it fall. Looking into the mirror she saw, behind her, Mave tie her own wiry hair into an identical bun, and fix it in place with a cloth ribbon. She tied another ribbon there, making a secure crisscross pattern.

She moved over to the wardrobe. She stepped into it, closed the doors, and a moment later emerged wearing a greenish gown the color of limestone with copper threads woven into it in a shimmery pattern. Woven also into the fabric were groups of iron coins that tinkled when she moved. On her feet were slippers made of dark fur with a large ruby on each toe, like toenails. When she was finished admiring herself in the mirror she said in an important voice, "Come. We haven't a moment to lose."

Annah followed Mave down the winding stairs that led to a damp basement where, through the high arches, she saw the red river that flowed into the distant mushroom forest. Another set of stairs led down to a stone dock.

Three canoes decorated with a royal crest in the shape of two white pillars stood in the still water. The mist hung low to the river and seemed to take on its color, and Annah felt as though she stood in the middle of a cloud of autumn leaves that had crumbed into dust and floated on the air.

 A boatsman dressed in brown skins bowed to Mave, all the while staring at Annah. She felt his eyes on her hair. With a grunt, the boatsman helped Mave and Annah into one of the canoes. Annah sat next to Mave and watched as the boatsman shoved off, scraping an iron pole along the rocks.

 The canoe was wider than it had seemed and was covered with a dark waxy material that repelled water.

 "You will take us to the Gallery, Jova," Mave commanded.

 The boat rocked through the water, past torches poking up from the hillsides. As though summoned, the Iterians came and sat by the river and watched as the boat made its way downstream. The trolls waved to the canoe and Mave nodded.

 It was apparent to Annah that Iteria was indeed heavily populated, and that by comparison Haza was stark and barren. The crowds cooed and smiled, and Annah waved to them. She pictured herself in queenly robes, seated on a throne of solid gold, acknowledging her subjects. The thought quickly vanished when she noticed Mave's look of boredom.

The boat took them a long way down the river, past fiery forges, through coppery haze, between granite hills that rose up on either side. It was hard to tell, with the mist and all, whether the river was sinking lower or the hills were becoming mountains.

The air grew warm, and Annah felt sleepy as the boat rolled through the thick water. When she yawned loudly Jova removed a dark fur from a box in the front of the canoe and offered it to Annah. She sunk into the fur like it was a pillow and watched the drifting landscape of reddish clouds, at home with this substitute for sky. Before long she closed her eyes.

꿍꿍

Annah awoke to the shrill sound of a train whistle and the smell of burning coal. From her seat in the train she looked around. The train screeched into a busy station with a glass dome. Outside it was raining and the rain came down like gray needles on the glass. People milled about on the platform wearing long coats, carrying luggage and umbrellas. Annah peered out the train window and wondered where the people were going. On the platform, a vendor sold cheese sandwiches and coffee.

 Annah wore a red wool coat with black embroidered trim, and on her feet were brown goulashes covering fur-lined boots.

 A hand touched her sleeve and she turned to see, sitting next to her, a woman with lavender eyes and hair the color of polished mahogany. Annah was surprised she hadn't noticed her before. She remembered the woman now, Mrs. Atherton from the orphanage. For a second, looking at Mrs. Atherton, Annah saw her own face reflected back.

 "We're here, Annah darling," Mrs. Atherton said gently, patting Annah's mittened hand.

 "Yes, Mother," Annah heard herself say. "I can hardly wait to meet my cousins."

ಶಿಲ

She awoke to a quivering yellow light and Mave's face in focus, bent over her.

"We're here, Annah," Mave said, repeating the dream words. "We're here, yes."

Annah blinked her eyes and leaned forward. They were passing through the mouth of a low shadowy cavern, and ahead were dozens of twinkling lights. Slowly the cavern opened up and she saw before her a village made entirely of sparkling colored glass. Annah, speechless, wondered if she was still dreaming.

They climbed out of the boat and onto a stone jetty.

A small crowd of onlookers awaited them, ooing and aahing.

"That's right, she is a human," Mave said in a possessive way.

Annah, still woozy from sleep, allowed Mave to take her arm and lead her along the path. The world before her lay shimmery and slightly out of focus, as though it was underwater. Annah took a deep breath.

They walked on the path until they came to a tall rectangular building of icy glass, frosted and spidery-veined.

Mave led the way as they entered through the heavy doors and into an open courtyard three stories high, everything made of glass.

Annah sucked in her breath and spun around.

"This region is known for its glass blowing," Mave said. Her voice, high and sparkling, echoed in the high ceiling. "Haza has nothing to compare with this, our Gallery."

Annah followed Mave through the courtyard. The area was decorated with glass sculptures, set out on pillars or attached to the walls. Behind the walls, the framework of the structure could be seen. Even the beams were made of glass.

Annah marveled at one after another fluid sculpture. A delicate troll girl sitting on a rock caught her eye. Some of the sculptures were inlaid with rubies and emeralds and iron. A ship made of iron had delicate riggings that looked like white threads. There was an entire mushroom forest—miniature—made of pale orange crystal streaked with gold.

Mave stopped in front of a set of tall glass doors, and pushed them open.

The room they entered was lined floor to ceiling with books sitting on glass shelves. The smell was familiar, and Annah smiled. Ink, and old paper, and the musty smell of leather jackets and dust. The room was not quiet like a library should have been; Annah thought she heard breathing, and small, muffled words.
Characters in the stories whispering to her. She became dizzy.

At last she said, "Where did all the books come from?"

Mave replied, "Where do you think? From ages and ages..."

"So the humans have been coming for all time?"

"I don't know. Perhaps. These volumes, many of them ancient, came mostly from Haza, smuggled here for safekeeping."

"Safekeeping from what?" Annah asked.

"From trolls who don't like books, I suppose."

"Why keep books if you can't read them?"

Mave smiled. "Sometimes the wizards can pick out a few words. Besides, now you are here, yes."

At one end of the room was a glass wall that looked out to the river and let a red glow into the room. It reddened the books, and the walls and ceiling.

Annah walked around and tried to see everything in the room. The room was divided into three separate levels or balconies. There were books on every subject imaginable, including cookbooks, and children's bedtime stories. She felt comfortable. She realized she had missed books terribly, and information in general. Reading was a way of keeping track, she supposed, keeping track of her life, since she had no clock, and probably no chance of going home.

"Do you think you could find the book?" Mave was asking.

"Oh, yes, the book," Annah said, letting her eyes roam across the room, and from ceiling to floor. She sighed. "Is there any rhyme or reason to the books here, I wonder?"

"Let's begin up there," Mave said, pointing to the topmost level, where a long row of books stood on shelves. "I believe they are the oldest ones, yes."

Annah looked up at the place where Mave pointed. The books looked as though they had been there for centuries—faded to pale, dusty colors. "Like finding a crumb of dirt on a mountain," Annah said, and began to climb the iron ladder that led to the top.

· TWENTY ·

Rud paced the floor, his chest heaving with each step. His heart was tired, and each beat seemed to drain more strength from him. "I do not believe you," he told Mars, who strode beside him in the grand throne room. "I do not believe my second son would betray me."

Mars reached into his pocket and took out the blue stone. "Then what is this, Father?"

Rud felt his mouth flinch as though he had been struck. He moved to the Chair of Light and sat down. He gripped the arms of the nicon Chair until the veins in his arms bulged out like brown worms. He remained quiet for many moments. "I am ready to sleep," he said.

Mars tossed the stone up and down in his hand. "I knew he wouldn't kill it. He's too weak."

Rud shook his head. Eelin had never lied before. Now Mars was another matter. "Where is he now?"

Mars smiled. "The Duots captured him just outside Iteria."

"And the human is obviously alive, but where..."

"Iteria, as far as I know. She escaped with that pig traitor, Jaden."

"The Army of Iron," Rud said, rolling his eyes up at the ceiling. The roof was inlaid with a mosaic of the Battle of Thenon, where he had lost over 50 trolls to Modoc's Army. He had always prayed to the gods he would never have to confront his brother's army again.

"The Army of Iron doesn't have Duots," Mars reminded his father as if reading his thoughts.

"But they have magic, you fool! Fally. And perhaps," his voice faded. "Winspur."

"I think we should take Mave, and then we'll find out how bad Fally wants her back," Mars said. "Take her..."

"You are more foolish than I ever dreamed," Rud said disgustedly. He could not stand the idea of relinquishing the Chair to Mars, this son with no wisdom. But Eelin had betrayed him. Both sons a disappointment. What a terrible season, he told himself. He closed his eyes. His heart felt like a cold nicon blade had pierced it.

"So Father, what do you intend to do about Eelin?" Mars asked in a taunting voice.

Rud didn't answer. He didn't know what he would do. He knew what he should do. The law dictated that Eelin should be calcified.

"Father, I will find the human and kill it, and then the stone will dissolve, and then I..."

Rud opened his eyes. "And rule Haza with a foolish heart," he said.

"And unite the kingdoms," Mars went on. "The Iterians are weak and we are strong."

"They are more than a thousand and we are barely a hundred," Rud finished.

"But they will listen to Mave. They will do what she says. As their Queen and soon to be Queen of all..."

"Ha! She hates you, Youngest," Rud said. "She will not have you."

"She could learn to care for me," Mars said, smoothing his pewter-colored hair. "I have never wanted for females."

"She is promised to Eelin," Rud warned.

Mars laughed. "She can visit him in prison. Besides, she hates Eelin just as much as she hates me."

"She is young and does not know what she wants. But what difference does it make now?"

"If only that miserable Fally were out of the way," Mars muttered. "I know she could be happy with me."

"You have always wanted her, haven't you?"

Mars nodded. "We are alike, Mave and I. Both strong."

"Stubborn and foolish."

"Better than weak."

Rud laughed, and his laugh turned into a deep cough. "Be gone from me, and do not fail me the way Eelin has."

Mars made a small bow and turned to leave.

"Aren't you forgetting something?" Rud asked.

"What is that?" Mars asked.

"The stone," Rud said. "I will have it."

"Very well." Mars tossed the stone to Rud and turned to leave. But he paused just before the door, head tilted. He whirled around. "I do believe our weary traveler has returned."

Voices sounded in the hall, and a moment later, the Council leader appeared at the door. Mars stepped aside as two guards brought in Eelin, bound in leather straps.

"Release him," Rud commanded, "and leave us alone."

The guards did as they were told. Mars stood at the door, arms folded.

"You, too," Rud bellowed.

Eelin stood in the middle of the room, silent, bloody, and pale.

Rud could not look into Eelin's eyes. He coughed, and the force rattled the bones in his chest. He looked at his second-born son, so different from Mars. So mild and without word. The task I gave to Eelin, to kill the human, was a fitting way to mark passage to the age of wisdom. I wondered if he would rule with a strong hand. Now I will never know.

Eelin stumbled forward, his feet bound by straps.

"You have betrayed and shamed me," Rud said in a voice that surprised him in its restraint. But his face was hot with anger, and his chest heaved with each breath.

"You would not understand," Eelin said quietly.

"You do not want to rule Haza?"

"You have no idea what I want."

"You deliberately lied..."

"I had every intention to do the deed," Eelin said. "But once I saw her, I could not."

"Weak."

"And I could not close the passageway forever. It is wrong."

"I will tell you what is right and what is wrong!" Rud stamped his foot, and his hand went to his throat, gasping for air.

Eelin crossed to his side. "Father, you are ill."

Rud pushed Eelin away and sat down on the Chair. How could he care for me, and yet betray me? he wondered. In his hand the stone felt warm. He held it out for Eelin to see. "You betray me for this?"

"I could not kill," Eelin said, hanging his head.

"Do you know what must be done to you?"

"Yes."

Rud pounded the arms of the Chair furiously. "You risked this for a human? You are as foolish as that brother of yours."

Eelin raised his head humbly. "The human is the last, the passageway is the last." He gestured with his chin at the stone. "It is the last. Its power is greater than we imagined. The Chronicler says the stone, the Saqa, can change trolls so that they can see..."

Rud spat. "To be like a human?" He clenched his fist and shook it at Eelin. "Are you ashamed of what you are?"

"Not ashamed, Father," Eelin said. "But to walk in the human world is to gain wisdom..."

"Haza is not good enough?"

Eelin did not answer.

"You have disappointed me," Rud said hoarsely. He could not put into words the worst of what he felt—that his son, the son he had lived for, would never be king. He could not bear to think of it.

Eelin turned his face away.

Rud took a faltering breath. "Mars will sit on the Chair, you know."

"I know, Father."

"There is nothing I can do. It is the..."

"I know."

Rud gazed at Eelin, too tired to deny the truth any longer that his second son possessed wisdom, true wisdom; moreover, he was the exact likeness of his beloved Hela. The anger drained from his body as he leaned back in the Chair and gave up the power that ruled his body. "I cannot help you..."

Eelin bowed in respect.

Rud bowed his head in return, and took his heart's last breath.

· TWENTY-ONE ·

Te guards were on Eelin in a moment. He had stood still, waiting for them to take him. He had looked at his father and seen his entire life, his failures, wave before him like a blanket of cloth. A deep pain clutched at his gut. I have failed him, he thought. For a moment he wished he had killed Annah which only served to confuse his thoughts.

Mars shrieked, "You have killed our father!" He slapped Eelin's face with all his might, knocking Eelin to the ground. When Eelin looked up Mars's eyes were glassy in their rage, but soon they became hard and cold as a Duot's.

Eelin looked at Mars with pity. "You have never cared about Father. Why do you pretend to now?" His voice was rough, like that of an old troll.

"Ha! You have never cared about anything but humans," Mars hissed. "You were never fit to sit on the Chair and everyone knew it." He moved to the Chair and pried the stone from his father's hand. He took the necklace of human teeth from Rud's neck and tied it around his own neck.

Eelin looked at the guards who held his arms in their strong grip as they pulled him to his feet. "Take me away so I don't have to look at his wretched lying face," he said. He had been saving these words to use once his father was dead. He had always pictured himself saying them while sitting on the Chair, with Mars standing before him, in shame. He continued, "You will rule in ignorance just like..."

"Just like Father? Go ahead, say it."

"It is not right," Eelin said, knowing his words were meaningless. "And I said, ignorance, which means—"

"I know what the word means," Mars snapped. "Father was not as ignorant as you think. But then you were too absorbed in your silly dreams of sunsets and rainbows to notice."

"You know nothing of my dreams."

"Come," Mars said. "Let me show you something in Father's chamber. Something I think will interest you." Mars nodded to the guards who pushed Eelin out of the throne room and down the wide hallway to Rud's chamber. The enormous room, decorated in animal skins, was the largest in the Hall. In the middle of the room stood an enormous iron bed with a head board shaped like a flame.

Mars moved to the stone wall and felt along it, pressing on one of the stones. The stone slid open to reveal a secret opening and he withdrew a golden box. Inside the box was an old book, part of a book, tied with a black leather strap.

Eelin stared. His heart beat wildly as he watched his brother untie the strap and open the crumbling book. He could not read the words, but he knew what it was, what it must be. The Book of Saqa.

"Father's book of poetry," Mars said with a wicked laugh.

"Mother's book of poetry," Eelin corrected him, playing along. He prayed Mars didn't know it was the Book of Saqa.

"Oh, but he could," Mars said, eyeing him shrewdly. "He could read as well as any human." Mars turned to a page where a deep red flower was painted. Words encircled the drawing. "Once there was a flower," Mars said in mocking tones. "A pretty red flower called the Saqa."

Eelin's heart sank. Of course Rud had the book. How else could he have made the Way? But now Mars had the book.

"You didn't know your own father," Mars jeered, tossing the book to the floor. The spine crumbled and broke, separating what was left of the book into three pieces. "And now he's dead and you'll never know him."

Eelin stared at the broken book. All this time my father could read, he thought. But how? Who taught him?

"Take him away," Mars commanded. "Let's see him chase sunsets from the crypt."

· TWENTY-TWO ·

After leaving Iteria, Jaden and Fally had gone straight to Modoc's cave. The Army of Iron had been summoned and they had advanced toward Sagpine. Jaden and Modoc had split up just before reaching Sagpine, each of them leading part of the Iron soldiers.

As Jaden and his soldiers passed by Sagpine with its yellow torches, Jaden thought of the Chronicler, which naturally made him think of Annah. He smiled at the privilege of having known her, but felt sad that he might never see her again. "I have the wisdom," he said, half to himself, and half to the gods. "Now that I have known a human."

Splitting up the Army might have been a fatal mistake, Jaden thought. His troop of 70 trolls were better trained than his father's, but they were weary. The food had run low. Worst of all, the messenger sent to speak to Modoc had not returned.

"Something foul is in the air," Jaden said, walking ahead of the Army to peer out past Thenon at the geyser plain beyond. They had made it safely through Longdeg, and at Thenon they would meet up with Modoc and Fally. After Thenon, it was an easy journey through the geyser plain and then Far Light Meadow. But now, he had a sick feeling that neither army would reach their destination.

Something felt wrong. Something smelled wrong. He listened from his post behind the rocks. Just yonder were the very rocks where he had slain a Duot, one of two who had followed him and Eelin and Annah as they traveled to Iteria. "This place is cursed," he muttered.

The flapping of a wing sounded in the distance and Jaden instinctively turned and ran back to the encampment.

"Swords out!" he commanded. His eyes were met by tired, listless ones. "Duots may be among us," he said. Without further words he directed his Army to break into groups of five or six and gather near the largest boulders in the area. He pointed to his nostrils in an exaggerated fashion; this reminded the trolls to use their sense of smell to locate the Duots. They are none too bright, the Duots, he reminded himself.

But they are invisible.

A familiar stench came just then, and he stood fast. A Duot was near, and it was directly to his left. He waited, counting one, two, three. He thrust out his sword and withdrew it. It was covered in purplish blood. He struck again and his blade pierced deeper.

He stepped back as a fallen Duot came into focus.

Behind him, the groans and shrieks of his Army sounded as they were attacked by Duots.

"They appear to be circling us," Jaden chanted, half-heartedly. "But we are many and we are clever."

Within a short time a dozen Duots lay on the ground slain. Two trolls in Jaden's Army were wounded, but not seriously. They were quickly bandaged by the caring ones.

Jaden motioned with his blade for the Army to run, sword-swinging, toward the temple of Thenon. It was not terribly far away, and what's more, the Duots would find it hard to strike moving objects making their way to safety.

The atmosphere grew dark with red smoke as they ran, which made it better. "Thank the gods," Jaden whispered, "we are making the Duots as blind to us as we are to them."

The Army reached the temple without loss of life. Quickly they entered the temple. They stood inside, breathing, resting, listening.

Jaden stepped outside the temple to watch and listen while his trolls rested. He closed his eyes. "We have made it this far," he said. "We have been attacked by the invisible and have prevailed. The gods are with us."

What happened next came as a complete surprise. An attack of soldiers, Mars's soldiers, without Duots, appeared, swooped upon them and soon had the Army surrounded in the Temple. Blades were out, and Jaden found himself warding off soldiers of the Royal Guard.

There must have been twenty of the guard, in all. Wherever did Mars find so many? Jaden asked himself. Were some of them Iterian traitors? Twenty is no match for ours, he thought. But six of them had found him. Alone. Six Royal soldiers who know how to wield a blade. The terrible realization struck him that the mode of attack was to kill the leader first. Kill the leader and it would destroy the Army. "Kill me," he managed to choke out. "It's me."

He took a slice to his gut, but rather than slowing him down, it made him wildly angry. Screaming, he thrust his blade into the soldier closest to him, and the Royal troll fell with a grave wound to the chest.

Jaden whipped around to face the other five. A second blow cut deeply into the muscle of his forearm. He thought of Eelin. "My friend!" he cried, and threw himself upon all five, slashing and screaming madly. "It must be!" he shrieked, not knowing why he said the words.

· TWENTY-THREE ·

Too much time passed in Mave and Annah's world. Jaden and Fally had arrived safely at Modoc's, word had said so many rotations ago. But nothing since then. As for Annah, how long she had been here in Iteria, she didn't know for sure. Days and nights and weeks were one. Only in her dreams were the days and nights separate, and only in her dreams did she feel unafraid. She often escaped to the safety of a book so she wouldn't worry about Eelin.

"Do you think Eelin is still alive?" Annah asked Mave each new rotation.

Mave replied, without looking into Annah's eyes, "How should I know?"

Annah became increasingly angry until one rotation she finally said, "Isn't there anything we can do to help? You're supposed to be Queen. Don't you care? What kind of Queen are you?"

Mave said nothing, but later that rotation Annah overheard her summoning her Governor and demanding that he send messengers to Haza to gather any news of Jaden and her grandfather, and to find out what had happened to Eelin.

Meanwhile, Annah spent time in the Gallery looking for the Saqa book. She had not found it, but she had found other treasures. She especially loved the books on troll lore and magic and, while she did not understand the magic, she read the books anyway. And she read to Mave.

Mave listened attentively to everything that was read to her, while keeping Annah busy returning to the Gallery to look for the Book of Saqa. Annah began to doubt the book would be kept in such an obvious place. But she went there anyway, sometimes with Mave, sometimes alone. She brought back piles of books to read to Mave. Classics, fairy tales, history books, geography books. Even cookbooks.

As Annah read, Mave became more and more interested in humans, to the point where Annah began to wonder if Mave had become obsessed.

When they were not reading together, Annah and Mave went among the trolls and Annah became quite popular with them. Soon entire troll families came to visit, pounding on the castle doors, wanting to talk to Annah, wanting to know about human life. And Annah could not travel anywhere without a group of at least ten trolls approaching her, stroking her skin, asking her how her hair came to be such a wondrous color. Annah would sit down right then and there and tell stories, any kind of stories, and they would listen, wide-eyed. It was so much like the orphanage, Annah thought, looking around at the trolls hanging on her every word, drinking in everything she told them.

Once Annah shared the book she had brought from home. First she explained how she had arrived in Haza. *"Adventures on the High Seas,"* she said, holding up the book to the young trolls who sat around her on the river bank. It was as though the book held the key to the human world. Trolls one by one touched the book, kissed it.

She had sat down and the trolls had assembled around her, on the damp ground, as she read a beautiful, haunting story, called *The Girl and the Scarf*, about a girl who lived on a great ship, but longed to go home. She wove a magic scarf that would take her anywhere she wished. She floated all around the world and settled in a kingdom called Zubibi, where the animals talked and where there had never been death or war.

When Annah had finished reading the story, she looked up to see Mave among the trolls, sitting still as a statue, tears streaming down her cheeks.

Later, in Mave's chamber, sitting in a chair in front of the fire, Annah turned to Mave and said kindly, "I could teach you to read. I've taught many of the children where I come from."

"So that is what a teacher does, yes," Mave said, leaning back in her chair and hugging her knees.

"I taught at an orphanage, which is a place where children live who have no parents."

Mave looked into the fire. "I have no parents."

Annah smiled. "Neither do I." As she looked at Mave's face, she was struck with the thought that Mave was like a small child.

"My parents traveled to Haza to speak to Rud about the unification," Mave began in a sad voice. "My mother was carrying me in her belly. They became ill in Haza. My father died quite suddenly, but Mother managed to return home. I was born early, and she lived long enough to name me." She managed a smile. "And now I must rule as true heir of all of this land."

"I know," Annah said quietly. "And you don't seem happy about it."

"I have no desire, no," Mave said. "For all I care, Fally can rule. Fally and Eelin can rule the kingdoms as one. It's what they've always wanted."

"And what do you want?"

"I don't know," Mave said. "Sometimes I think I don't belong here."

Annah nodded. "I know what it's like not to fit in. You could move to Haza," she suggested.

Mave made a face. "Never would I live there, no." She looked hard at Annah. "Tell me once again what it is like in your world."

৪০৪০

At last word arrived from Haza. Mave had called a meeting of her Advisors in the Chamber Hall. When the meeting was over she came to speak to Annah in her chamber.

"Rud is dead," she told Annah breathlessly.

Annah rose from her chair. "Dead?"

"And Mars has imprisoned Eelin and sits on the Chair."

Annah closed her eyes tight to stop the tears.

Mave stood staring blankly at her hands.

"The Army of Iron has advanced beyond Barden and have split into two armies," Mave said. "The messenger said he has spoken to Modoc himself who will meet up with Jaden just before Haza. They are in need of provisions, especially good water. And they could use more swordsmen."

"I'll go," Annah volunteered.

"All the Iterian forges are making swords," Mave said. "We are preparing for war with Mars. It is as prophesized…"

Annah broke in, "Perhaps I can help with the training. I have killed a Duot. I can wield a sword. A little."

"How did you learn?" Mave asked.

"From Jaden himself," Annah answered.

Mave had an odd, confused look on her face, as though she did not believe Annah.

"I will do what needs to be done," Annah said finally.

Annah began, the next rotation, by visiting the forges in Iteria, helping to load swords for transport to Barden. A hundred swords were gathered and sent off by mules, while hundreds more were being cast for the Iterians who would be leaving soon to help Modoc and Jaden. Annah would be traveling to Barden as soon as possible, leading a small army. She had been surprised that her idea to lead the army was met with no argument from the Iterians.

Meanwhile, she set to work teaching the Iterians all she knew about sword battle.

Along the riverbanks they gathered for lessons. "I don't know anywhere near what Jaden knows, but I can help," she told the Iterians. Male and female, young and old trolls had volunteered to learn the sword, in order to help the famous Army of Iron. They all wanted to fight alongside Jaden and Modoc. And they wanted to please Annah.

One early rotation, Annah sparred in front of the mirror. Her sword gleamed in the candlelight and she cut a fine image of a troll soldier with her leather dress and belt. "This is what Mave should be doing," she muttered. "What kind of Queen is she that she doesn't want to help her people and rescue Eelin?"

She went to Mave's chamber to tell her that she was leaving for her sparring practice. She paused at the threshold of the room. Mave lay sprawled on the rug in front of the fireplace, a golden beaded slipper dangling on one foot. She pored over Annah's book, stroking the pages and gazing longingly, saying the words aloud as her finger followed the words. Either she had taught herself to read, or she had memorized every single word in the story about the girl and the scarf.

· TWENTY-FOUR ·

Annah prepared for her journey to Barden. She, along with 120 Iterians, would be leaving the second rotation after sleep. Her preparation was more mental than physical and she couldn't sleep. *What have I got myself into?* she asked herself as she lay staring up at the ceiling, perspiring.

They drank tea in the copper eating room. They ate an early meal of bread, and roasted tubers with rare herbs. Annah felt an odd longing for Mave to come along, as though having her would bring luck. Of course, Mave should stay behind. She was needed at home, even if she provided minimal protection and care for her people. Still, Annah found herself saying, "You can come along if you wish."

Mave said, "I hate war. Besides, I have a people to rule, yes."

Annah heard herself say, "Most of your people are with me." She smiled. "It's best you stay here."

"I will miss your stories," Mave said.

"I found something you might be interested in," Annah told her. "When I was at the Gallery last I brought some books, and one of them tells of a great war in the human world. Wait, I'll get it."

She went to her chamber and returned with a heavy black book. "Sit and I'll read a chapter to you," Annah said. She began to read, and the story was one of knights in shining armor and fair maidens in flowing gowns. There was a three-headed dragon slain by a brave knight in the name of the beautiful Princess Liliana of Portugal. The princess loved Sir Phillip who had slain the dragon, but before they could marry he was killed by a jealous knight who also desired her hand in marriage.

"Wasn't that an exciting story?" Annah asked when she had finished.

Mave sat in an enraptured silence. She put her palm to her cheek at last and said, "The beautiful gowns and the magic looking-glass that would speak to Princess Liliana! Oh, I wish I could live that way."

"It's only a story," Annah said. "In the human world there are many wonderful stories. There are many here in Iteria." She patted Mave's brown hand. "I could teach you to read. I know you would like to learn." She was curious to see how much Mave knew already. "Here is the letter "A", see?"

"You, your body is full of stories, full of words," Mave said bitterly. "All the letters look the same to me." She paused. "You have words, yes. But you have no magic."

"No magic," Annah repeated.

Mave sighed. "I would not mind being Queen if I had trunks full of gowns, and perfumes and... and horses to ride."

"It is a beautiful land where I come from," Annah said. "But there is no magic. There is a certain kind of magic in the green rolling hills, and snow, and trees, and birds, and libraries, and churches, and zoos and..."

"You must miss it terribly," Mave said.

"In some ways I don't," Annah said. "Because I never really had a family. All I had were the children. So there didn't seem a place for me."

Mave nodded. "I have only Fally."

"In my world," Annah said, "a person can be adopted by a mother and father if you don't have them."

Mave raised a thick brow. "But you were not adopted, no."

Annah bit her lip. "No. I didn't want to be adopted. Because I knew my real parents were alive. Somewhere."

"And they did not want you?"

"Maybe they couldn't take care of me. Maybe they lost me. Headmistress Downing says that sometimes parents are unfit to take care of children, especially when they themselves are barely children. But it doesn't mean they don't love them." The last words brought a tear to her eye, because she suspected they applied to her own life, and that perhaps

Headmistress Downing knew who her parents were all along. Annah didn't tell Mave the truth: that there were too many children and not enough parents.

"It must be nice to be human," Mave said in a quiet voice.

"You don't want to be a troll, do you?"

"I have always known in my heart that I was meant to live someplace else."

"You should have faith, Mave." She looked at her own tired face reflected in the copper table and said, "Your subjects are counting on it."

⛧

Annah helped load the mules for the trip. There were seventeen in all. None of them had Salt's quiet disposition, though they were stout.

The food had been stuffed into packs and hung from the mules, and Annah's "Army" of Iterians stood at attention, bursting with enthusiasm. Half were young female, and the other half were male, young and old.

Annah stood in front of the Army, sword at her side. "It's almost time," she said in a faltering voice. I have never done this, she thought. And they know it. Surely they must be laughing to think of me as their leader.

She held out a torn leather map showing Barden, Sagpine, Thenon, The Geyser Plain, and Haza, with Far Light meadow bordering it. She smiled, remembering the meadow's pale colors and how she felt when Eelin returned, how glad she was to see him. "Our orders are to travel to Barden and wait," she announced. The Army nodded.

No sooner were the words out of her mouth when she looked up to see Fally walking down the hill, alone. Annah knew something terrible had happened. She ran toward him and saw the look of failure and sadness on his face.

"Are you wounded?" she cried, as soon as he was within ear-shot.

"It's no good," the old troll said. "No good at all."

Annah felt the blood drain from her head. "What's wrong?" she asked, grabbing his arm.

"Jaden has lost his life," Fally said. "But his soul lives."

A terrible sigh came from Annah's throat. Her legs went limp. "It can't be. He is the best swordsman. It can't be. He was so…"

"The Duots were larger in number than we could know," Fally said, taking her arm. "We barely made it out of Sagpine."

"But I thought you were waiting for us in Barden!" Annah cried.

"We advanced and were attacked."

Annah put her hands over her face so Fally would not see her tears. "Jaden is too good to be dead. Only bad people die."

"My magic wasn't strong enough," Fally said angrily. "I could make the Duots visible, but there were too many of them. And now the Army has many wounded, and Modoc is heartbroken. Without Jaden nothing matters to him."

"We can fight the Duots," Annah said fervently. "I have slain..."

"Let's go back and think about this," Fally said. "They are smarter than we thought. We will summon deeper magic. You and me, Annah."

The two of them made their way down the hill toward the castle. When they reached the army assembled by the river, Fally said to Annah, "Let me take them, you go on ahead, child. Check on Mave and I'll catch up."

Annah returned to the castle to find Mave sewing by the fire. Annah faded into a chair and stared into the fire and said nothing. Soon Fally came into the room and hugged his granddaughter.

"The war is over?" Mave asked.

"No, it is just beginning," he said. "I am sorry to say that Jaden is dead." He smoothed Mave's hair.

Mave snorted. "What a terrible waste, this war." She glanced at Annah disapprovingly.

She looks at me as though it were my fault, Annah thought.

· TWENTY-FIVE ·

Mave sat in her chamber, staring out the window at the Andor River. She could not stop worrying about Eelin. She had said yet another prayer to the gods, one that appeased them and apologized for her life's mistakes, and begged them to keep him alive. She had not gone so far as to want to trade her own life for his; she could never do that. For although she was betrothed to him, she had never planned to marry him. Not him or any troll. But still, she cared. More than she would admit to anyone.

And what would happen to Iteria? she wondered. Will Mars send an army of two-headed monsters to kill us all? "Am I to die?" she asked the river. "I could travel to Haza. I could persuade Mars to end the fighting. Mars has always desired me, yes," she murmured, looking at her pale lavender nails filed to petal shapes. She smiled. "He would do as I tell him."

Six rotations later, Mave quietly slipped away while Fally and Annah were at the Gallery. They had gone to search for books of deeper magic and would be gone for at least two rotations—time enough to pack a mule and steal away.

Mave had left word with her governor, in the form of a drawing on moth silk. The drawing was a self-portrait and above it a flame, which symbolized that she had gone on a royal mission. She commanded him to tell no one where she was going. She had never before traveled to Haza without Fally, but she felt safe enough with her trusted maid Win, and with the nicon sword at Win's back. Unfortunately, neither of them knew how to wield it.

She had donned her most fetching cape of pink-tinted rabbit and had placed golden rings on every finger. She combed her hair and tied it into a bun with three ribbons that were studded with rubies. Mars will not be able to resist me, she told herself, remembering the princess from the story, the beautiful princess whom the knights fought duels over. She tied a golden scarf around her waist to make her waist appear smaller.

She snuck away, riding the mule, with Win walking alongside. Win was younger and did not complain about having to walk. She did not complain for she did not like to be struck.

During the trip, Mave thought about Annah. What a curious strange thing, that human, she told herself. She was at first indifferent about the human, but now she found herself wanting to be like her. She certainly wished she could have a little of her bravery. But this is my own brave deed, she reasoned. After all, there could be Duots at any turn.

"I am going to rescue Eelin," she told Win.

Win looked at her and nodded, and tugged on the mule's lead. "That is good, my Queen."

"Mars will be glad to see me, yes," she bragged. She did not tell Win the real reason she was going to see Mars, one that she did not dare speak aloud, for fear of someone lurking, listening. But she intended to take the crystal.

And the reason she wanted it had nothing to do with Eelin or Annah.

ಬಂ

They arrived in Haza, exhausted, Mave complaining, and were met by guards before they were a half-league from the Hall of Souls.

Mave lifted her hand, open palmed. "I come to see Mars," she called out in a proud, queenly tone. "Take me to him at once. And feed and water my mule."

Mave and Win were escorted to the Hall, and taken straight to the throne room on the upper floor. "Wait outside for me," Mave told Win, as she stepped into the circular room. She had not seen this place since she was a child. It gave her an eerie, frightened feeling, and she began to doubt whether or not she could do the deed at hand. She tried not to think of her parents, tried not to remember that they had died after coming here.

Mars arrived within the rotation, grinning, and swelling with self-importance, Mave thought. She had not seen him in many hundreds of rotations, not since his journey to Iteria when they both were small. He had not changed as much as Eelin had in the same length of time. He was still thin, too thin. His smile was the same: without sincerity. And his eyes were still cold.

"Mave, what a pleasant surprise," he said. "You have grown to be more beautiful than I remember."

Mave put out her hand and he took it in his for a moment and then placed it to his cheek. "Let's go to a more private place," he said, leading her to the adjoining private chamber. The walls of the tiny room, inlaid with rubies, seemed to radiate warmth. The floor was strewn with silken pillows. A canopy of gauzy cloth hung from the ceiling. Mars showed Mave to a padded bench and they sat down.

"I am so glad to see you," Mars said. "I did not expect you to come in this dangerous time."

"I had to come."

"Why?" he said cautiously.

"Now that the Prince is imprisoned, I thought it only fitting.

"What do you mean?"

Mave's brow shot up. "You have never seen the look in my eyes?"

Mars gave a start. "I had no idea..."

Mave put on her best smile. "I've cared for you since we were infants."

Mars grinned, and touched her hand. Then his smile twisted into a frown. "That brother of mine did not care for you like I do."

Mave frowned. "No?" She wondered if this was the truth or if it was simply Mars's truth.

"He was more concerned with duty, and that ridiculous idea of keeping human contact."

"What do you intend to do with Eelin?" she asked quietly.

"I think I shall let him rot in the stalactite prison," Mars said. He looked at Mave questioningly. "Or do you think something else should be done?"

She gave him a look of disdain. "Why don't you make him work in the forges instead? It seems a degrading enough task. Keep his foot chained to the wall like a dog."

"I have thought of that," Mars said.

"Or let him serve the Duots, yes," Mave suggested.

"It would be easier to let him rot in the crypt," Mars said.

Mave showed her displeasure by turning her head away.

"Does that not please you, my Queen?" Mars asked.

"It's just that I see no reason to kill him," Mave said. "And besides," she said, patting his arm, "it would make you seem cruel to your subjects. The Iterians are not used to such barbaric behavior." She said the word Iterians without emotion, as though she herself were not one of them, but rather a Hazan.

Mars stroked his chin. He smiled. "Does this mean you intend to..."

Mave smiled coyly. "With Eelin in the crypt, my betrothal to him is hardly binding."

Mars nodded. "Hardly. And besides, I perceive he is in love with the human. He must be, or he would not have spared her life. Can you imagine that? A troll in love with a human?" He laughed wickedly, his eye-teeth showing white and sharp.

Mave laughed too. "Such rot," she said, her voice faltering. Inside she began to burn with jealousy at the thought of Eelin having feelings for Annah. True, she herself had not been kind toward Eelin, and he had respected that, kept his distance, but he had asked for her hand willingly. She looked at Mars. "I wish to proceed with the ceremony."

Mars bowed his head in thanks. "It is true then..."

"Oh yes," Mave said. "Very soon, yes." She looked down her eyelashes at him. His nose was too small and sharp and his hair was too well-cared for. His clothing was clean, too clean, and so were his nails. It sickened her.

"We do want to unite the clans as soon as possible, don't we?"

She jerked her head back slightly. "I will marry because I wish to. <u>Not</u> to cement alliances."

"Exactly what I was thinking," Mars said, reaching for her hand. He gazed at her longingly. "I had no idea you felt so about me."

Nor I, Mave thought.

"We will be a strong ruling force."

"Yes, yes," Mave said. She gave him a sideways glance. "Especially with Eelin in prison." Where he can rot, for all I care, she thought.

"Yes, with Eelin in prison," Mars said absently. "I must summon the servants to make my wedding clothes." He looked at Mave. "And you shall wear a red gown of the finest moth silk, with a thousand rubies worked into the design."

"Oh that would be lovely, yes," Mave said. "And I could wear the stone around my neck as a symbol of our love," she added quickly, nodding, twisting the rings on her fingers.

Mars shrugged. "Anything you wish, my beloved."

"I wish... I wish you would stop," Mave said in a bored voice. "Is all that silly fighting really necessary?"

Mars said nothing, but continued to look at her adoringly.

"And what about the pathetic little human?" Mave asked. "Annah, she is called. What shall we do with her?"

"By all means we should kill her," Mars said.

Mave nodded sweetly. "By all means, yes." She turned her face to him and let him kiss her on the lips. She held her breath and fought the urge to gag.

· TWENTY-SIX ·

After the late meal, Mave was taken to a lavish guest chamber on the main floor, just down the hall from Mars's chamber.

"I wonder where he is keeping that stone?" she asked, wringing her hands. She stood in front of a great gilded mirror, studying her face. She tugged at the hair at her temples and watched as her eyes tilted upward at the corners. "Tie this hair up securely, Win," she commanded. "I'm seeing him again this very rotation. I need to look my best."

"You don't really plan to steal it, do you?" Win asked, doing as she was told. She made a tighter bun in the hair, and straightened the beads on Mave's dress.

Mave turned and gave Win an exasperated look. "Of course I do, why do you think I've come here?" She smirked. "You don't think I actually intend to marry that pompous fool, do you?"

Win shook her head. "Stealing the stone would be more than dangerous, my Queen."

"Don't worry, I'm not going to take it until the time is just right." Her eyes narrowed to slits. "If I am careful, I won't have to steal it. He will give it to me."

"I think it is unwise, my Queen." Win smoothed Mave's hair with a silver comb.

"This rotation I will go to his chamber, yes," Mave began in a confident tone. She smiled at herself in the mirror one last time before she turned to leave. "And when I return I will have the Saqa stone in my possession."

She walked down the hall a short distance and rounded the corner. A door at the end of the hallway stood partially open and she crossed to it.

"There you are, Mave," Mars called from inside. "Please come."

She entered the chamber to see him rising from a grand chair at the foot of the bed. They embraced and he kissed her cheek. He smelled of myrrh and clove. On his head was a thin crown of nicon. A chill ran through her when she saw the crown that was meant for Eelin.

She moved to the window that looked out on Lake Mered. She looked out the window briefly, then let her eyes slowly roam the room. The rabbit pelt-covered bed stood in the very center of the room, and beyond that, an enormous closet with two open doors revealed rows and rows of magnificent clothes. The sight of the clothes gave her a slow, sickening feeling. More clothes than my own, she thought.

"We have many things to discuss," Mars said in a voice that was both gentle and excited.

"Yes, my King," Mave answered automatically. She smiled demurely. "The wedding ceremony will be a splendor."

Mars crossed to where she stood and took her hand in his. "I want you to have the ring my mother wore."

"Yes, of course," Mave said, glancing around the room discreetly, looking for the crystal's hiding place.

"You won't mind removing one of these then?" he asked, touching the rings on each of her fingers.

"Oh, these are nothing special," Mave said, waving her hand.

"The stone is rare amethyst," Mars said.

"Oh, I do love stones," Mave said. "Especially blue stones." She stroked his forearm.

Mars gazed into her eyes. "In that case, you will love the Saqa." He rose and went to his bed table and opened the drawer. Inside the drawer was a gold box. He carried the box over to Mave and handed it to her. "Look inside," he said.

Mave opened the box to see the oval stone. She gasped. "Oh, it's remarkable!" she said, picking it up. "I cannot believe how lovely it is." She held it to her neck, conveniently bare of necklace. "Oh, do you think we could have it fixed to a chain?" She bit her lip and bounced on the floor. "Oh, I would love it so!"

Mars smiled kindly. "Of course we can."

"When?" Mave asked. "I cannot wait to wear it! I could give it to my good smith at the forge…"

"Certainly before the ceremony," Mars went on.

Mave put on her best smile. "And I hope it is soon, my King."

"So do I." Mars took the stone and placed it back in the box and put the box away. "Let us waste no time, then," he said happily. He held out his arm for her to take. "I will call a special meeting this late rotation. I will make the announcement to the Congress of Light and we will begin with the plans."

Mave took his arm and he led her to the door. When she crossed the threshold she glanced back at the night table in disappointment. No matter, she thought, I will have it before I leave for Iteria.

ಬಂ

"Win, I need your help," Mave announced, as soon as she had returned to her chamber.

291

Win was sound asleep, snoring.

"Wake up, stupid troll!"

Win's eyes popped open.

"I need you to distract Mars while I slip into his room."

Win shook her head. "My Queen, I am hardly a good liar," she said groggily.

"Oh, posh, you can do it," Mave said. "Tell Mars you wish to consult with him about something important concerning me. And once you get him alone, tell him I was too embarrassed to ask what kind of sleep robe he would like me to wear on our wedding night. Talk about the wedding gown. What was it he said? Something with rubies. Ask if he prefers a long flowing gown, or one of thick folds, or one cut low in the front. He could talk for a season about clothes, the fool. Ask him how he would like me to wear my hair. Discuss the dowry, and anything else you can think of relating to these matters. You can do it, troll. You must!"

Win made a sour face and wrung her hands. "I will try, my Queen, but I have never married, and I know nothing of these things. Please try not to be gone long."

"Don't worry," Mave said. "I'll get the stone and we can be on our way."

"All right," Win said, rising from the bed. "I will go to him now."

"Good, you do that," Mave said. "He's still up in the throne room with his ridiculous governors."

Win left with a small bow. Mave cautiously stole down the hall to Mars's golden chamber door. She turned the knob. It was locked. She crept around the corner, to where she suspected the servant's entrance must be, to the small door that led to the closet. There were two wooden doors there, side by side. The first one was locked, but the second door opened when she turned the handle. It led straight into the room where soiled garments were kept. At the end of this tiny room was another door, which she opened, and found herself amongst the fine clothes in the closet. "The gods be thanked," she said. "It is meant to be."

Peering through the vast rows of clothing she saw the iron posters of Mars's bed. Not a sound could be heard in the chamber. It lay empty except for a cat sleeping on the soft bed covers.

She tiptoed across the marble floor and to the bed. She opened the bed-table drawer, opened the gold box. The cat meowed and she stopped and glanced at it.

"May the gods protect you," she said with a slight bow of the head. She took the stone from the box. Just then there came the sound of the outer closet door opening.

"Oh," she groaned. "Where will I hide it? I know." Quickly she reached up to her hair and pulled the bun apart. She tucked the stone inside the hair and tightened the cord that held the bun. She threw herself across the bed and began to stroke the cat.

The maid entered, carrying an armload of fresh bed clothes. When she saw Mave, she let out a small gasp.

Mave put on an embarrassed look. "I was expecting..." she began sheepishly.

The maid set the clothes on the bed. "Sorry Ma'am," she said, giving Mave a knowing smile. She ducked out of the room the way she had come.

Mave wiped the bead of perspiration from her upper lip. She glanced at the open bed-table drawer and went to it. She reached inside and closed the golden box. As she began to close the drawer, something in the drawer caught her eye. Under the gold box was a book, broken into pieces and tied with a leather strap. Mave withdrew the book and opened it. It was ancient, and it was decorated on each page with a small scarlet flower. Mave's heart pounded wildly as she tightened the strap around the book and stuffed it down the front of her gown.

She groped in the back of the drawer, looking for more treasures, but there was nothing else there. But when she pulled the drawer open further and looked again, there was something in the back of the drawer that caught her eye. It was a small pouch, butter yellow in color, and soft from wear. It looked familiar. "This must be important or it wouldn't be here," she said, stuffing it down the front of her dress. And with that she bid a good life to the cat, and slipped out of the room and down the hall to her chambers.

Win returned a short while later, breathless. "Did I give you enough time?" she asked.

"More than enough, yes," Mave said. She had packed her things already, putting them into the leather travel bag. "You will go downstairs and announce our departure. Tell the servants to fetch provisions."

"But no sleep?" Win asked in a disappointed tone, picking up the bag.

"I will tell him I am too excited about the ceremony to sleep," Mave said. "I'll promise to be back in 28 rotations. And I will seal the promise with a deep kiss. "That should make the fool happy."

Win, shaking her head, went downstairs to the servants' chamber.

Mave went directly up to the throne room, where Mars sat on the Chair, speaking urgently to his chancellor. Mave bowed slightly at the door.

Mars murmured something to the chancellor, who promptly left. "Mave, come," he said, waving her inside.

She strode gracefully to the Chair. "My Lord, we have prepared to leave, and will return in 28 rotations, if that pleases you."

Mars stepped down from the chair and took her in his arms. "You will not sleep?" he asked, pouting. Mave felt his hot breath near her ear.

"I am too excited to sleep," she said, giggling. She shook her head slightly, bent still closer to him, and the scent of her lin berry perfume filled the air.

Mars held her close. "My Queen," he whispered. "Your journey has been too brief."

Mave brushed a kiss across his lips and said in a sultry voice, "I do have a people to rule, Mars, my love."

His face reddened at the sound of his name spoken. He pulled her closer and kissed her until she pulled away with a sultry smile.

"Until then, Mave, my love."

Before he could say another word she slithered out of his arms and crossed the room.

She paused at the door and looked back to meet his gaze.

"My journey has been brief, true, but fruitful beyond my wildest dreams." She giggled as she hurried down the corridor and took the stairs two at a time down to the Hall foyer.

· TWENTY-SEVEN ·

Mars stared in horror at his image in the chamber mirror. He was shocked to see that the recent evenings' banquets had added size to his middle. "No food for 100 rotations, " he muttered. Not a difficult task. He could do anything if he had to. If he wanted to.

As a young troll Mars was confident and determined, and sure of who he was, even before he could speak. He was sure of who his father and brother were, too. He watched them out of the corner of his eye and thought them both fools, opposite though they were. He was especially disappointed in his father. He could be stronger, Mars thought. Eelin, well, he was hopeless. He would never be king or anything else. Mars was sure that Mave, Princess Mave (the only troll he could stand) would never marry Eelin. What could she possibly see in him?

As he studied his form in the mirror he pictured Mave as his Queen, sharing his bed, and it made him shudder with excitement. At last she had come to her senses with her broken promise to marry Eelin. She said she'd always desired Mars. He hoped it was true, hoped that it wasn't just because Eelin was in the crypt. He and Mave had so much in common—they were so much alike, right down to their taste in grand clothing and food. They even saw eye-to-eye on the matter of the human. They would have a good life together.

He thought about the human, the girl called Annah. "What will we do with her?" he asked the mirror as he fingered his ruby necklace. "The teeth might do well between these rubies," he said. "And how many teeth does a human have?" Fewer than trolls, but he was not sure how much fewer. The idea of actually wearing Annah's teeth had a sudden odd effect on him that he did not expect. As though it was wasteful—not because she was the last human, no, but because it might be interesting to have her for awhile instead of killing her. It was not uncommon for royal trolls to have both a mistress and a wife; Mave understood this, and would surely not mind. Rud had refused Hela's gift of a human—his hatred for them was too great—but other trolls throughout history had had human females. Now that Rud was dead he could do as he pleased. He could do anything he wanted. The notion of taking the human as his mistress, the girl Eelin cared deeply for, would die for, made him grin.

"Annah," he whispered. He liked the sound of that name.

· TWENTY-EIGHT ·

Mave and Win arrived safely in Iteria. No Duots chased them, and the stone stayed securely in Mave's hair. "Best place for it," she had said. The yellow pouch she had opened the moment she felt safe to do so. She had almost cried when she saw that it contained a tiny seed. She tied the pouch to the book at its leather strap.

"I hope there is enough of the book," she had said, glancing at the faded pages, and at the paintings of flowers and seeds and stones. She even recognized the word "Saqa" written at the top of the page which bore the large diagram of the flower. She knew these letters, this word, stood for the flower. "Saqa," she told Win. Win had looked at her blankly. Mave tucked the crumbling book back inside her dress as Win watched. "What if we are robbed?" Win had fretted, shaking her head. Mave had silenced her with a wave of her hand.

Mave and Win arrived at the palace to find Annah and Fally seated at the copper table, deep in discussion. Mave couldn't wait to get to her chambers. "I've returned," she announced gaily as she swept up to Fally.

"Granddaughter, you are safe!" Fally cried, rising out of his chair to greet her.

"Of course I'm safe," Mave said, removing her outer cloak and handing it to Win.

"You were foolish to travel to Haza," he said sternly. "You could have been killed."

Mave's hands went to the bun on her hair, centering it, making sure the stone was safe. "I'm here, aren't I?"

"But why did you leave?"

"I went to Mars to plead with him to stop the fighting," she said. "And he said he would think about it."

Fally's eyes narrowed. "And what did you promise him in return?"

"Not much," Mave said. "But I am tired and wish to rest now." She glanced at Annah, who smiled weakly. The poor human, she thought. Probably still brooding over Jaden's death.

"Mars is not to be trusted!" Fally said desperately. "Even if he swears on that miserable soul of his, he is not to be believed."

Mave kissed her grandfather on the cheek, being careful not to bend down too far so that he would see the book still stuffed into the bosom of her dress. "I must sleep. We'll talk when I am refreshed."

She bustled up the stairs to her room and stood in front of the mirror. She adjusted her hair, felt the stone. "How lovely my hair looks," she said with a smirk. She removed the pouch from its hiding place, took out the stone and held it up to the mirror. "Soon I will learn of your power, won't I, yes?"

She carefully withdrew the book. She opened the large nicon jewelry box on the table next to her cot and placed the treasures inside. She locked the box with a little gold key which she removed from its hiding place under the cot, then strung the key on a long chain and hung it around her neck. Then she put on her bed clothes and went to sleep.

༶༶

The first rotation after sleep Mave went down to the eating room to join Annah and Fally.

"Granddaughter, are you all right?" Fally asked. "You look a bit sad. I will go to my chambers and get my medicines."

"No, I am well," Mave said, forcing a smile. "Please don't bother yourself."

"Nonsense," Fally said, and whisked out of the room.

As soon as Fally was gone, Mave turned to Annah. "Did I tell you the good news?"

"What good news?" Annah said.

"Mars has <u>promised</u> that he will not kill Eelin."

"And you believe him?"

"He gave me his solemn oath."

Annah sat very still in her chair. "He is alive then?"

"I saw him myself. And he asked about you, yes," Mave said kindly.

Annah smiled and there were tears in her eyes.

"Dear, it is all right," Mave said, patting Annah's sleeve.

"We must help him!" Annah said fiercely. "Jaden has died. To surrender to Mars is to believe he is right."

"You really do care for him, don't you?" Mave said.

"I love him," Annah said in a trembling voice.

Mave sucked in her breath. A chilling, jealous wind enveloped her. Although she did not want Eelin for herself, she did not want Annah to have him either. Before she could stop herself, she blurted, "How interesting, since we have been betrothed since childhood."

Annah's face fell into sadness, but she seemed to quickly regain her composure. "Fally will rescue him," she said after a moment.

Mave smiled. "I'm sure he will rescue him, Annah. And then the war shall be over, yes. And now I must go to my chambers." She was weary of the war talk. She climbed the stairs to her room, amazed at how boring Annah seemed, now that she possessed the crystal, the book, and the seed. Everything seemed boring. "I have the key to the human world," Mave told herself with a smile.

She took the book from her jewelry box, and plucked the seed from its pouch. She held the seed between her two fingers, to the light. It was such a tiny seed. "I shall grow a most exquisite flower," she said. "Oh, I cannot wait to see the human world. And who says trolls cannot learn to read?" She turned the stiff pages of the book. "Saqa," she chanted. She turned a page of the book to see the large flower, with the crystal in the center of it. The center of the crystal had an eye drawn there, and the eye looked up to a human sun. "Interesting," Mave said. "Very interesting. Yes."

· TWENTY-NINE ·

Eelin bent forward, on his knees, in the murky cell where the stalactites dripped down onto him. His upper arms were bound to his sides by iron shackles, and around his waist was tied a chain that held him close to the wall. His black hair, usually braided with golden threads, now hung loose and wild and filthy. He was of course without his belt, his blade, and his precious pouch. Of all his possessions it was the lock of Annah's hair he missed most. "If only I could touch the lock of hair," he whispered. "It would give me strength as I prepare for sleep."

Slowly the calcium and lime had begun to encrust him in a stone prison where he could not move, or even feel his legs. "So this is what it is like to be a stalagmite," he said with a bitter smile. "I am part of the earth, without brain, or heart, or feelings." His blood ran through his veins cold, like the water that slowly fell onto his head.

"If only I had more of the magic in me," he said, shivering. "But wishes are no good." He thought of Annah, pictured her gentle face as she awoke from the dream about her mother. He wiped the thought away, saying aloud, "And that is how I shall remember her, and that is the last."

And then he prepared himself for death's sleep. "I have failed," he whispered to himself. Never had he known such cold of body and soul. His feet were without feeling and he bent forward, rocking back and forth to keep warm. "If I am to die like this, it is my own fault," he said.

He dozed off, and dreamed he was a bird that soared up and out of the passageway, into the human world. The bird touched clouds and went right to the sun before it came back down to the passageway and into his world. Once in his world he saw a girl, but it was a strange girl:

half troll, half human. The girl resembled Mave in the face and body, but she had Annah's hair, and her strength.

The door to the cell creaked opened, and Mars stepped in.

Eelin shook himself awake.

"How are you, brother?" Mars drew his rabbit skin robe to him. "A bit cold, are you? A bit disheveled? Your hair is a mess, brother. Too bad. You look so small and insignificant without your necklace and princely robes."

Eelin gave him a hateful look. "The Army of Iron will come to my rescue," he said quietly.

"That is doubtful," Mars said, putting out his hand to collect a drop of lime. "But I have not come to talk of war and killing. I have come to talk of love."

"You know nothing of love except for the love you feel for yourself."

"I am betrothed to Mave," Mars said, flicking back his hair. "She has professed her adoration for me."

"I do not believe it." Eelin looked straight ahead, chin up, and tried not to show the sadness welling up inside him.

"It's true. We have made the announcement to the Congress of Light."

"Mave despises you."

"She has apparently changed her mind about me," Mars said. "She has matured to marrying age, apparently. She sees the value of uniting the clans."

Eelin furrowed his brow. This was highly unlike Mave. It was common wisdom that she was not interested in marrying, and that she had no desire to rule. She must be tricking Mars. But why? Is it to rescue me? he wondered. "And will she love you when you tell her that your idea of unification is to enslave her people? Will she love you when you tell her that?"

"It will happen so gradually she will not even notice," Mars said, gazing at Rud's gold ring, loose on his slender finger. "Besides, her kind are all so passive anyway."

"Except for Mave."

Mars sighed. "I'm sorry you won't be able to attend the wedding. It will be a glorious event, I am sure. I will drink a toast to your, um, growing stalagmites."

"Get away from me," Eelin said. "Mave will never marry you, and you will get what is coming to you." His stomach churned with jealous rage.

"I have everything coming to me," Mars said. "Did you think you could win? Really, brother? I will kill you, and that horrid human. I will sit on the Chair. Oh, I almost forgot. Thank you, brother for giving me the Chair."

Eelin squirmed in his bindings.

"And when you take your last breath, picture your human friend's teeth around my neck." And with that, Mars left.

"I am going to die here," Eelin whispered. "I never should have let Annah live. This is what I get for being good, and doing what is noble." He quickly said a prayer to the gods to undo the words. "Perhaps it is good that Mave is marrying Mars," he said in a whisper. "She will not let me die here, will she? She will persuade Mars to set me free. She must have some feelings of duty, mustn't she?" He tried not to believe the words Mars had told him. He tried to believe what he had grown up to believe, that he and Mave were meant to rule the trolls. One kingdom, one king and queen. He prayed to the gods that she at least cared about him.

He glanced up as an icy drop touched his nose and hung there for a moment before he shook it free and it struck the floor. A green and orange encasement had begun to climbing up his legs. His hands were free to knock away the stuff that clung to his body, but only that which he could reach; eventually he would be covered with the gritty material. The blood to his legs would stop, and the legs would die. He would die. Slowly.

He examined the cuffs on his feet. He stared at them, willing them to break apart. He couldn't stand the thought of dying with them around his feet. I will sleep a Royal sleep," he said. "For I have a soul." The words died in his throat as he lost consciousness.

· THIRTY ·

Annah stood in front of the mirror, holding her blade, the only connection she had to Eelin. On her cot lay a book she had been reading that contained magic incantations. She had helped Fally read them; he had had helped her sing the incantations properly, in the right tone of voice and inflection.

"We will walk in the land of the darkest caverns, neither troll nor human, neither flesh nor blood but alive still. Spirits, with souls..." This was the magic that moved flesh from the awake state to the dream state.

Eelin and Jaden said I had the touch, Annah told herself. She stared at the book and envisioned Eelin alive, marching to Iteria, leading his father's army, and the Army of Iron as well.

She sat on the bed. She opened the book to the second to the last page, which described communication through water. She read the brown ink words, in a chant. "Taste of this, and color the water's sparkle with fingers." She went to the water basin next to her cot and stared into it. She dipped a finger into the half-filled basin, set a drop on her tongue, and stirred the water until it coursed in a small circle.

"Eelin, I long for your face in the water's magic." She sang the words three times. The water was supposed to act like a communicator. Slowly an object came into focus. Was it a stone? A stone with markings, and something else. No, it was a face. Dark eyes, closed, dark hair sticking to a wet forehead. "Eelin, can you see me?" Annah asked. The figure vanished, but Annah was sure it was Eelin.

Annah's heart began to thump. Is Fally right? If so, together they could use magic, and if their magic was strong enough they could free Eelin from his prison. And if that didn't work, she thought, looking at her sword, I will personally slice Mars into bite-size pieces and feed him to the Duots.

　　She hurried down the stairs to meet Fally in the eating area, which they called "the room where magic is born." Fally smiled when she entered the room. Mave stood looking out the window, and turned to look at Annah briefly. Even in that small glimpse, Annah detected, in Mave's shifting eyes and twitching lips, a secret. Mave had been acting odd since her return from Haza. She had been in her chamber most of the time, not even coming out to eat. Something had happened to Mave while she was in Haza. But Annah didn't have time to worry about that now. Perhaps after Eelin was free she would turn her thoughts to Mave.

　　Annah sat down at the copper table. "Fally, I saw him in the water, I saw Eelin's face! And I can feel my magic growing stronger. If we put our magic together, we could both become invisible and free Eelin from prison."

　　Fally smiled. "Getting in is one thing, but getting Eelin out is quite another. It isn't as though he's standing around waiting for us to open the door. He is most likely in poor health, perhaps close to death."

"He's got to get out," Annah said. "He's got to take the Chair from Mars and unite the clans."

"It was always meant to be," Fally said solemnly.

"I wish I could help Eelin rule the clans," Annah said without thinking. We could..."

From across the room Mave glared at Annah. She turned and hastily climbed the stairs to her chamber.

Annah watched her disappear, then looked blankly at Fally. "But I thought she didn't want to rule..."

"Child, child," Fally said, patting her hand. "Did you not know that Mave is promised in marriage to Eelin?"

Annah felt her face grow hot, and a lump formed in her throat. Of course she knew, and of course, it only made sense.

"Didn't you know?"

Annah shook her head yes. "But Mave doesn't care for him."

"She is fickle and immature."

"She doesn't love him," Annah said angrily. "She doesn't care if he lives or dies."

"Still," Fally said, "it is ordained."

"He will never marry her," Annah said. "Never. I am sure he does not love her."

Fally smiled. "Eelin will do what is best for the trolls," he said. His face grew sad. "And Mars will do what is worst for the trolls." He paused. "Eelin can certainly use whatever help you can give him."

"I've been practicing the incantations," Annah said. "We can make the entire Army of Iron invisible, and we can make Eelin invisible and remove him from prison. We can enter the dream state together, Eelin and I."

Fally looked thoughtful "Invisible? The entire army? No. Eelin, it might be possible. But... there is a poison made from purple zynna plant, and it can be blown across the air to cover the enemy. One whiff of the sweet, heavy scent and they will sleep for a hundred rotations. But first you must know the enemy is there."

"You really are a wizard, aren't you?" Annah said.

"I have learned the magic that was always here, taught to me by my father. It is only a matter of choice to know which magic to use and when." He looked hard at her. "And you have magic in you, passed down by your parents. But perhaps in your world it is not called such. Perhaps in your world it is called wisdom."

"I don't know who my parents are," Annah admitted. "But I have dreams of my mother. She has lavender blue eyes."

"You will find her, I am sure."

"I won't ever get home, will I?"

Fally said, "I am a wizard and yet that is a question I cannot answer. You will always have a home here with us."

"I feel as though I've come here for a reason," Annah said. "I think that by coming to your world, I will find my mother. Isn't that odd? And I think maybe I'm supposed to help Eelin."

"It may be so. The army will assemble in twelve rotations. And we will use all the magic we have against Mars. I have my books to consult."

Annah translated the time in her mind. Twelve rotations was approximately 24 hours. "But I'm not ready yet," she said. "I don't have enough magic..."

"You are clever."

"You have the power to become invisible, Fally. That is true magic."

"Soon you will have the power, Annah."

༼༽

Annah and Fally stayed up until late in the rotation practicing chants. Annah learned how to control her breathing, and her heartbeat. Once, when she went into a trance, she became part of a dream, but at the same time outside the dream, watching herself.

As she saw her face looking back, the face of a woman with lavender eyes and dark red hair came into focus next to her. "Mrs. Atherton," Annah heard a voice say, and she was not sure if it was her own voice, for the Annah she watched did not move her lips. "Mother," the woman said. "Mother," the voice repeated. Annah put her hand to her lips, and felt her own mouth speaking the word. The images faded, and was replaced with Fally's image. In her mind's eye, she saw herself and Fally rising up, floating through the castle walls and hovering in the air above the tallest turret.

Annah saw another image, at Seton House, and all the children were gathered around Headmistress Downing, who was talking to them in excited whispers. The day was warm and they were out on the grassy lawn. Annah watched herself as a younger girl, among the children, images flashing by quickly. The girls wore their summer white dresses and lace-up boots as they played jump rope, while the boys in their best shorts—all hand-me-downs, of course—played with a ball. In the sky, birds drew circles and the sun threw shadows across the lawn.

Annah looked closely at herself, the plain little girl with short hair (she'd found the scissors and cut off her long hair so it wouldn't hurt so when Miss Downing combed it). The dream Annah sat alone at a picnic table, watching the children, stroking Abbi's dress. A cake stood on the table in front of her with five candles on it. As Annah watched herself she was surprised at how serious and inward she looked. She had always remembered her childhood as being pleasant and happy; she had never wanted to grow up.

The image faded, and Annah was brought into a third place. Out on a dark, wet plain she stood, along with Eelin. A chilling wind blew her hair.

As Annah watched, Eelin smiled at her, while behind him a Duot stole forward, with outstretched talons. She saw the Duot, but Eelin did not. "Turn around, turn around, Eelin!" she screamed. But Eelin did not hear her. He continued to look at her serenely, filling his eyes with her. Annah found she could not take her eyes from his. She had seen the look his eyes gave her but now, from this perspective, she saw the look as something else, yet still familiar. She had seen this look in her dreams when the eyes were not great brown troll eyes, but blue lavender, and the eyes were full of love.

Eelin continued to look at her and she realized that he was oblivious to everything else around him. The Duot's taloned hands snaked out and in an instant, Eelin's neck was caught in the creature's clamp.

Annah fell to the ground, heaving, breathless. She looked up to see Fally standing over her.

"What is it child?"

Annah choked, sick at the realization she had come to. "I know why Eelin was taken," she said. "I saw it, in a vision. He wasn't thinking. He wasn't paying attention. He was looking at me."

"Looking?"

"More than looking." Annah took Fally's outstretched hand and stood up to face him. "He was looking at me and I know his thoughts were completely..."

"He was consumed," Fally said. "He was no doubt concerned with your safety and his will was locked into caring for you. That is why he left himself open to the attack. Oh, I have much to learn."

"If he had been thinking about Duots, if he had been expecting them, concentrating, he would have sensed them. I know he would have."

Fally's pale eyes widened. "That is what we will do," he said. "We will instruct the Army, teach them to keep their thoughts free of all things except for seeing Duots. Expecting them."

"Do you think it will work? That we'll see them?" Annah asked.

"We will sense them, if not see them. But we won't know until we get there," Fally said. "We have our magic, we have our weapons. All we can do is hope."

ಚಿಖ

It took a long while to plan for the journey and pack the supplies. They set off a rotation early and met up with Modoc and his army just outside Sagpine. They were over 300 strong, with Fally, Annah, and Modoc in the lead. It felt strange to Annah for Jaden not to be there. Annah wore battle skins over the white leather dress Mave had given her. Wild black hair had been woven into her own. She did look scary, she thought. Troll-like.

Out on the tunnel road they were silent. Annah tried to focus on Duots, and most of the time she was able to, but often thoughts of Eelin would creep into her mind and she was powerless to push them away. The road was as silent as the army, and there was a cloud of fear that seemed to follow them.

When at last they reached Haza and the spot where Annah had first come, she stopped, and could not help herself from staring at it. As the army rested she ventured close to the alcove and looked up. It was not the dark, terrifying place she had seen when she was pulled through by Eelin. It was a peaceful quiet spot and not at all dark. She looked around at the rocky walls, and down at the ground. "Why was I so frightened?" she wondered.

She could see perfectly now, as if the cavern was lit by many torches. "How wonderfully amazing," she whispered. She squinted up to see the toy box that she knew wasn't there. So far away her world was! She strained to hear the sounds of the children in the nursery. She wanted to whisper, "Headmistress Downing, I'm here, in Haza. And I'm all right.

Look inside the toy box." She wondered if they had patched up the hole in the box. She wondered if the hole had always been there, or if it had been there briefly, magic brought by the Saqa, the hole in the toy box sealed the moment Eelin took the stone.

    Annah and the army stole along to the grotto, and began to assemble in front of the Hall of Souls. Lake Mered was black as Annah had imagined it would be. All was strangely quiet. Not a troll stirred anywhere. It was as though the entire village had disappeared.

    A tug on Annah's arm made her jump. Fally, looking bulkier in his battle skins, whispered in her ear. "When you hear the word we will split into groups and surround the Hall. Keep your eyes and thoughts on Duots. And say a prayer to the gods that the Duots do not take us now and tear us apart like chickfowl."

· THIRTY-ONE ·

Something unexpected happened. Mars, alone, dressed from head to toe in gleaming blue fabric, stepped onto the white balcony that rimmed the Hall of Souls. He stretched out his hands in a gesture of peace. He smiled, and even at this distance, his teeth gleamed white.

Annah could not take her eyes from him. How beautifully his hair shone. His skin was smooth and clean, his posture straight. He resembled Eelin in the shape of the face and the full mouth. He seemed kindly, not the cold-hearted troll she knew him to be. And how brave he is, she thought, to stand there out in the open where he could easily be pierced by an iron arrow.

From atop the stairs he said in a gentle voice, "Why have you come?"

"You are not the rightful heir to the throne!" Modoc shouted.

Annah murmured, "And you have killed Modoc's only child."

Modoc's words were echoed by the Iterians, shaking sword, bow, or dagger.

Annah watched Mars, trying to see more of Eelin in him.

"We need not fight like this," Mars said in a controlled voice.

"Give us back our king!" Fally shouted.

"So this is your army, old man?" Mars said, changing the subject. Or perhaps stalling, Annah thought. She glanced around, trying to conjure up the image of Duots. She saw and felt no danger around them. It was odd.

"Is that all you want?" Mars said at last. "Of course you can have him."

"How do we know he's alive?" Modoc shouted.

"I can prove he's alive," Mars said in a voice that faltered. His eyes traveled to the rear of the army.

Annah felt a sickening rumble in her stomach. Something was not right. She looked harder at Mars, and tried to figure out why he stood there so quietly, and where he was hiding his army. Next to her Fally whispered, "He is up to something. Look around you, look for Duots."

"I am," Annah whispered.

Before the words were out of her mouth the screams began. One by one members of the Iterian army began to fall, bloody, to the damp earth.

Annah looked up. Mars was gone.

At the same moment Fally turned to the ranks. "See the Duots. They are already among us!" he commanded.

Fally grabbed Annah by the shoulders. "You, go find Eelin now. Take that turn at the corner of the Hall," he said, pointing to the side of the Hall that faced the lake. "Go down the stairs, and always follow the right fork. We will fight here. Go now." Already she could hear the piercing cry of Duots falling and it gave her hope. Perhaps the magic was working.

Annah hesitated and searched his tired eyes. "Fight well," she said, and slipped away.

She kept her eye on the lake as she circled the Hall of Souls. "If only I could make myself invisible," she said, drawing her skins to her.

She had just found the side of the Hall and the stairway down when a taloned claw snatched at her neck. The pain was instantaneous, and blood began to ooze down her front. She stopped. She focused her eyes on the Duot she knew to be there. "I can see you, I can see you Duot," she chanted. Her heart thumped against her ribs. Her sword was out, an extension of her outstretched hand. "You are right in front of me, I can smell you. I can see you."

A shimmering form of gray began to appear, just long enough for Annah to plunge her sword forward. The Duot screamed, and took another swipe at her and managed to rip the fur from her shoulder. This wound was worse than the first, and Annah cried out. She ducked, withdrew her sword and plunged it again, into the image which was fading from view again. The Duot shrieked and fell to the ground, Annah with it. Now the Duot was fully visible and Annah knew it was mortally wounded. Her blade had plunged through the creature's stomach and into the earth.

She stood up and put her boot to the creature's middle and withdrew her sword.

She began to run downstairs, and from inside the stairwell she heard the terrible screams of both Iterians and Duots as the battle went on.

At the bottom of the stairs she found a stable door, which she entered. She stayed close to the wall sides and smiled when she saw a mule which looked very much like Salt. Straight ahead was a set of stairs which led to a tunnel made of gray stone blocks. A breezy chill set over her as she made her way along the tangle of passageways. She kept right, heading downstairs, around and around, then straight. She passed by a kitchen where a roaring fire blazed, unattended.

She passed by a set of doors which she did not open, and then the hallway abruptly bent downward, a steep decline, veering right, and she smelled a moldy, damp, creepy smell. At the very end of the tunnel stood a lime-encrusted door, and it was without the ornate carvings of the last set of doors she had seen. She knew this door hid a room of torture and death.

From beneath the door came a faint green glow. She paused to catch her breath. She put her hand to the door latch, pressed it, and to her surprise the door opened.

There, in the middle of a small room was Eelin, bent forward in an awkward, impossible pose, bound and shackled, and almost completely encased in lime. He looked like a statue.

· THIRTY-TWO ·

"My Lord," Annah whispered. She could hardly bear to look at him. Tears streamed down her face when she saw his matted hair and the chains wrapped around him, chains that stretched to the wall. As she neared him he opened his eyes and looked at her, and didn't seem to recognize her. His eyes were masked with a gauzy film.

Eelin put his head down. "Annah," he whispered weakly. "It's you."

"Yes, I've come to rescue you," she said.

"Save yourself, go away from this place while you still can." He wiggled his thumbs at her. His arms were bound at his sides.

"I don't want to go away," she said. How can I tell him I prefer this dark labyrinth to the horrors of Mave's splendid castle?

"Please go," he hissed.

"No, Eelin. I have learned magic and I can free you." She smiled so he would not be afraid, to show that *she* was not afraid.

"Go!" The circles under his eyes were purple and there were insects buzzing around his head, waiting for him to die.

"I know magic, I tell you."

"What kind of magic?"

"Magic that I learned in the books with Fally."

Eelin shook his head slowly. "No magic can help me. I am doomed, and you will be too, unless you get away."

"I can make us disappear," Annah said confidently, trying to convince him and herself.

"You cannot break these chains from me," Eelin said. "Your sword is not fine enough."

"Yes it is, because you gave it to me." She removed her sword from its scabbard and plunged it into the crusty earth. She placed both hands on the top of the hilt and wrapped her fingers around the sunburst. She closed her eyes and put herself into the invisible dream place she had found before. It was the world where her mother lived, where she herself lived in the past. And it was a place that was neither in the human world nor the troll world.

Annah imagined herself there, alone first, then with Eelin. "We will walk the dream world together," she murmured. "I call upon the spirits of the dead trolls whose souls lie beneath this room."

The sword in her hand shuddered and became warm. Annah, with eyes tightly closed, imagined herself and Eelin standing outside the door of the cell, him free of his lime encasement and bindings. "Just a few moments away," she whispered, hoping her words would soon guide them into the dream state. "We are there together, in the invisible place," she chanted. "We have left this prison cell and are outside its walls."

She was completely unaware of Eelin's presence in the room, and sensed only the Eelin who now appeared before her in her trance. He stood alive and smiling, in front of her and he reached his hand out in a petting way and touched her hair. She touched the hair on his face, and felt the soft stubble. She felt strangely thick and heavy of body, and at the same time buoyant.

She whispered, and her voice sounded distant, the way voices do in dreams. "We will leave this cell and enter the silent world of the nowhere. We will walk in the land of the darkest caverns, neither troll nor human, neither flesh nor blood but alive still. Spirits, with souls."

The sword in her hand grew warmer still and the room filled with heat. A shuddering pain went through her body, and she opened her eyes. She could not see Eelin. "Eelin," she called out in a desperate voice. Was he lost? Dead?

There was no answer.

Annah clutched the hilt harder, until she thought her fingers would bleed. "Take us to the other side," she commanded. "Trust in yourself," she whispered.

Slowly her body began to rise from the ground, light as air. The room swirled around her and she lost hold of the sword. A moment later she stood outside the prison cell, her feet planted on the ground. But where was Eelin?

Annah's hand went to her mouth to stifle a cry. She whipped around in the dim room, and felt a rush of cold air. "Where are you?" she whispered.

"Annah," a strange voice called. It was otherworldly.

"Eelin?" Annah asked. "Eelin, come to this place," she said. She reached out for the sword, to collect its dream form in front of her, but it wasn't there. One glance told her it was back in the cell room, still stuck into the ground. "I must have let go of it," she muttered. She needed the sword to complete the magic.

She once again closed her eyes and said the chant and stood, wrapped in her own silence in the trembling air. She spoke: "We will leave this cell and enter the silent world of the nowhere. We will walk in the land of the darkest caverns, neither troll nor human, neither flesh nor blood but alive still. Spirits, with souls."

The blade was once again in her hands. She concentrated on Eelin whole and well, standing before her, his brown eyes wide and questioning, his waist-length hair shining blue-black in the dim light. "Now," she whispered.

Eelin's warm breath came next to her cheek.

"Oh," Annah said, reaching out. She felt his face, and quickly her other hand took hold of his arm and held tight to him. He came into focus. The magic had worked, and she continued to hold him while he became solid flesh. "I won't let go of you," she said. Now they were standing outside the cell, wobbling as though coming out of sleep.

"Annah," Eelin breathed. He began to fall and she caught him. Although the shackles were gone and the lime no longer part of his body, he was terribly weak. "The stone," he said, as she helped him to his feet. They clasped hands and Eelin began to lead her down the dark corridor and up the stairs.

"You are not able to walk," Annah said.

"Mars's chamber," Eelin replied, pushing forward. "That is where I would hide the stone.

Under the bed or in the wardrobe, or someplace where nobody goes. And Annah, there is a book, I saw it, and the seed is there too, it must be." He stumbled as he tried to walk forward, and she caught him.

"How will we get in?"

"I have a key in my chamber," he said.

They found Eelin's chamber door and he reached down to his ankle, took a key tied there and opened the door.

He swept in and out of his chamber in a moment's time. "Mars was foolish to think I would live to use the key again," he whispered as he closed the door behind him. They crept down the corridor.

Outside Annah heard the battle cries. The air was filled with the smell of fire, scorching clothes and hair.

They passed by a troll on the way to Mars's room, and Annah flashed her sword. The young female let out a cry and ran off.

"Trust no one," Eelin told Annah after the troll had passed by.

They came to Mars's chamber and Eelin, breathless, opened the door using a small iron key hidden along the door's upper ledge. "Another foolish mistake, " he said.

Annah followed him into the room and Eelin closed the door silently and locked it. He put the key in his trouser pocket.

"You check all the clothing drawers, and I'll check the bed and clothes room," Eelin said. He tore the golden quilt from the bed and threw the thick under bedding to the floor, revealing iron planks.

Annah pulled open drawer after drawer, reaching her hand into the soft clothes. Then she went to the closet and pulled the clothes out, piece by piece, from their iron hooks.

"We must find the stone," Eelin said. "We must find it and the seed. And the book." He threw clothes into piles, muttering, sounding crazy, obviously from fatigue.

"What book?"

"My father's book, it tells of the Saqa's magic. We need it. To send you home."

Annah spun around. "Home?" she cried. "Home? I don't want to go home." The word had an odd sound to it. Like a word just learned.

He did not appear to be listening. "I was foolish not to send you back right away," he muttered.

"This is my home now," Annah said quietly, watching Eelin from the closet as he searched the room.

"We will find them," Eelin continued. "Mars cannot be allowed... I wonder if he has it with him," he rambled, after he had searched the bed and the dresser next to it, and opened the golden box in the drawer. The box was empty.

"He might have the stone on him," Annah repeated, still watching Eelin.

"No, he does not have the stone on him," came a steady voice from the darkness of the closet. Annah felt a sword on her spine as Mars stepped into the room, pushing her toward Eelin.

· THIRTY-THREE ·

Annah advanced carefully toward Eelin, terrified that she would stumble and the blade would rip into her. A small cry escaped from her mouth. "We've come this far, and now..."

Eelin pulled open the bed drawer and withdrew a dagger as easily as if it was his own room, his own blade. He pointed it at Mars and used the tip of it to nod. "Let her go. This is between the two of us."

Mars took Annah's shoulder and slowly turned her around to face him. He touched the sword tip to her neck. "I have never seen a human," he said, grinning. "She is quite remarkable, brother. No wonder you couldn't kill her. And what a lovely troll dress you wear. One of Mave's, perchance?"

"Let her go, it's me you want," Eelin said.

Annah steadied her eyes on Mars. His eyes were yellow, and shaped like a cat's. They moved from her to Eelin and back again. There was no emotion in them.

How could I have thought he was anything like Eelin? she wondered. He is so unlike Eelin. Rather dashing, she found herself thinking, but evil—it seemed to ooze from his amber eyes. She closed her own eyes to find the dream world, to make herself one with Eelin, to make them both disappear.

Mars brought the tip of his sword from her neck down her arm, and her concentration faltered. "I see you have all your fingers, pig human," Mars said.

Annah's eyes flashed open at the insult.

Mars laughed. "You fooled Father, but you did not fool me with those ridiculous stone fingers," he told Eelin. "Father's eyesight is feeble, but mine is sharp as daggers."

Annah spit on him. "You are a poor excuse for a prince," she said.

"I am not a prince," Mars corrected her, laughing. "I am king!"

The words were scarcely out of his mouth when Eelin, shrieking, jumped forward with his dagger at Mars's face.

Annah instinctively ducked and stepped out of the way. The two brothers were at once engaged in horrific combat. The sword and dagger clashed, making a terrible din, unlike anything Annah had heard in sword practice. The sound was like a metal file being dragged across a thousand metal rocks.

Annah clutched her throat to find her breath, but she couldn't seem to catch it. She pointed her sword to strike at Mars, but Eelin was suddenly close to her. She couldn't risk stabbing him.

Eelin's dagger was no match for Mars's broad sword gleaming in the candle light. Mars's sword sliced Eelin's stomach, and he groaned.

"You will never be king!" Eelin said, jabbing his blade at Mars.

"I will and I am," Mars sneered, stepping back.

Eelin lunged, wiped his dagger across Mars's face, cutting it, but only superficially.

With a howl, Mars jabbed his sword at Eelin, inflicting a gash to his arm.

"You are a human-loving pig!" Mars shouted.

"You are not good enough to call yourself my brother!" Eelin said.

Eelin's stomach and arm were bleeding, and his shirt, still green with lime, took on a peculiar mottled color.

Mars swung his sword high as he advanced toward Eelin.

Eelin cautiously moved backward toward the bed. He was a better swordsman than Mars, Annah thought, but he was acting crazy, as though he had nothing to lose, as though he wanted to die; he had already allowed himself to be cut twice. Annah knew it was only a matter of time before Mars killed Eelin. And then he would turn on her.

Annah sidled toward the clothes closet, trying to circle behind Mars. He turned to face her as she brought her sword gingerly out to her side. Eelin was near the bed now. He heaved with each breath like it was his last. He had probably not eaten in days. It was a wonder he had fended off Mars this long.

But it's two against one, Annah told herself. She stretched out her sword toward Mars, and he knocked it from her hand with one well-placed blow. He turned to Eelin, whose trembling hand clutched his stomach in an attempt to stay the blood flow.

Annah shuffled backward and her eye fell upon a statue sitting on a little shelf attached to the wall near the door. The statue was an iron bust of Mars, with a kingly crown on his head.

Mars sliced his sword at Eelin's arm once again, and Eelin cried out. The blood came out copiously and his shirt was instantly soaked.

Annah grabbed the statue, stepped up to Mars and lifted her hand to hit him on the head, but her foot was caught in the bed quilt and she fell to the floor. Instantly Mars spun around and thrust his sword at her. She rolled around, trying to extract herself from the golden bed cover.

Annah screamed when she saw the blade above her.

But Mars's sword stopped in mid-air. Annah looked up into Mars's face and saw a peculiar open-mouthed grimace, and his eyes were frozen in surprise.

Eelin's dagger had found its spot in Mars's side. As Eelin withdrew the blade, Mars slumped to the ground on his back.

"Where is the stone?" Eelin demanded as he stood over Mars. "Where is it or I will kill you now."

"Kill me," Mars whispered, clutching his bleeding side. "Go ahead and do it."

"Where is it?"

"Kill me, or are you afraid?" Mars laughed weakly.

Eelin kicked Mars's blade from his hand, knelt down and held the dagger above Mars's heart. "Where is the crystal?" he demanded.

Mars shook his head. "You cannot do it, can you?"

Eelin's arm did not move, it was poised in mid-air as though made of stone. He turned and looked at Annah, but the words were directed to Mars. "Unlike you and Rud I cannot kill my own flesh and blood." He closed his eyes, then opened them again. "Come, Annah."

She stood and together they went to the chamber door. Eelin put the key in the lock and opened the door.

"About the crystal–" Mars called out in a hoarse voice. He laughed.

Annah and Eelin paused and turned to hear what he had to say.

"You want the stone?" he said sarcastically. "Go ask that soulless creature Mave where it is."

· THIRTY-FOUR ·

The hardest part about the Saqa magic, Mave thought, was finding the right location to start it.

"It must be a place where human sunlight touches the flower and makes it grow," she whispered, remembering the drawing of the red-orange circle of light pointing down to the flower. "No toy boxes like Annah's Way," she said, remembering Annah's stories about coming to Haza and seeing Eelin for the first time. "No dark boxes, no."

Mave knew that it was chance, really. The lightest spot in Iteria would not necessarily be a light place in the human world. "If only the Saqa could find a field of human sunshine," she told herself as she stole along the tunnel road.

The Saqa plant she had started from the seed grew in an earthen pot, and a tiny scarlet flower poked up through dark leaves. The pot was kept hidden in her clothes chamber where it had bloomed in less than twenty rotations. Not even Win knew where she had hidden it.

Now she held it underneath her cloak as she sailed the Andor. The crystal was safely tucked into her waist pouch. "I must begin the Way in a place where nobody goes, where nobody would find it," she had said. She knew there were many such places in Iteria. "And if no sun finds the Saqa," she had reasoned, "I can always move the plant to another place, yes." She patted the flower pot, so small and easily transportable.

She reached the City of Glass, and instructed the boatsman to leave. "You will tell no one where I am," she said. "Or you will be punished." Her heart burned wildly as she made her way to the Gallery. Here was a place where she could hide the flower in a hidden corner on the top level. "No troll would ever think to come here," she whispered. "Nobody but Annah. And she will not be returning from the great battle in Haza. Not alive, no." She felt sad that Annah would not be returning. She had grown to tolerate her, even care about her.

She climbed the ladder that led to the topmost level of books, then pushed the rickety ladder along on its rusty wheels, and sent it flying across the room. She set the flower pot on the row of books and sat down next to it, her legs dangling over the shelf. The cavern ceiling was high enough so that she could stand.

She looked down to the Gallery floor, and across to the great glass window that framed the Andor. "The flower cannot be seen from the ground," she whispered. "I wonder how big the passageway will be." Her heart pounded as she recalled the word she had recognized in the book on the page with the diagram of the flower. "Saqa," she said. That word she recognized, but no others. But to be able to read this much. Surely she was special… a rare troll.

She knew she must somehow place the crystal into the plant, for the primitive drawings showed, not a crystal, but an eye in the center of the flower. The egg-shaped crystal was pale and clear just like an eye.

She reached into her waist pouch and took out the crystal. She looked at it, and she was afraid. Perhaps something terrible will happen, she thought. "Perhaps the sun will burn down into this place and I will die." She looked at the scarlet flower. "But I am dead already," she whispered. "Soulless if I stay here." She thought of her parents. "I will never see your wisdom," she whispered. "No."

Without another moment's hesitation she placed the stone in the flower's center.

Instantly the crystal began to glow pale blue.

Mave gasped. The flower brightened in color. Clearly the crystal was alive, as alive as she was. Though it had no eyes it turned to her, looked into her, and then it gazed all around the room. The many faceted crystal pointed itself to the glass overhead, and slowly a hole began to appear there, burning into the glass, fire without fire. Mave peered up into the space. Kneeling, she thrust her hand into the hole and felt the warm rush of air. "Where is it?" she asked the crystal. "What place is this?"

She saw in the hole a glimmer of light that seemed far away at first, but then became brighter. She sensed a dry air that clung to her nostrils. She stood crouched on the bookshelf. A sheet of blue light filled the hole. The light, though transparent as air itself, was a magic barrier, she knew, a thousand leagues wide, separating two worlds that could not be more different.

She thrust her head into the hole, through the blue light. What she saw took her breath away—it was a human sky with puffy white clouds. A sky, yes. The sky was a color she had never imagined. Her eyes began to tear at the intense light and she had to cover them. She felt sick to her stomach, and sat back down.

"It will never work," she said bitterly. "I cannot leave, no. I am being punished. I have abandoned my duty. And I have left Eelin to die." She began to cry. "I could have helped him. He was good and kind, and I left him to die." She bit her lip until it bled. "I do love him. But I am too young to marry. I have not yet lived out my child-life. I did not ask for marriage. I did not ask to be queen over a race of trolls, no. I want to read books, and ride horses, and learn to play the piano. And... and I want a mother and father. Moskuis," she said in the ancient tongue. "Sanwqii."

As she spoke, something strange began to happen to the flower. Fruit buds appeared on the plant, first one, then another. The fruit, blue and oval like the stone, continued to grow until the plant's leaves sagged with the weight. Mave could smell the fruit's sweetness. The fruit was like the food crops grown in the valley, but of a color not seen before. She touched the soft, plump fruit, and it fell into her hand. She brought it to her lips. It smelled of honey and spices, and of something magic and exciting and rare—so rare she wondered if she was dreaming. Perhaps the magic had entranced her.

"This is the magic, this is the magic, yes," she chanted happily.

Without another thought she took a bite of the wet flesh, and instantly a warmth rolled through her body. The fruit tasted delicious. She ate all of it, smiling as she was filled with its sweetness.

She peered up into the sunlight once again. This time the light did not bother her eyes. She looked, smiling, anxious to see all of the human sky without pain. She stood up her full height, and squeezed her shoulders into the hole, which was just large enough for her body. She peered around at the new world. She used her elbows to pull herself out of the hole to see better.

She sat on the edge of the Way, her feet hanging into the rocky passageway below. This sunny place was nothing like her world, which now seemed dark and sad.

She stood up. The blue sky was there, yes, and she stood in the middle of a field of huge yellow flowers, the biggest flowers she could possibly imagine. They grew on tall green stalks. They were strong-looking stalks, like stalagmites, yet they bent to her touch and they did not break.

The air was full of dust particles, and she sneezed. It was like stepping into a cloud of warm light and dust. The sunlight felt good on her head, and when she looked up, straight up, she felt her eyes change to let in the sunlight. She felt peculiar all over, prickly and weak. "It is the fruit that has given me sight. That, and magic, yes."

From her flowery meadow she saw distant hills, green as far as she could see. Like the best emeralds, huge and bright.

"It is more beautiful than Eelin could ever have imagined," she whispered, tears coming to her eyes. "If only he..."

"Hey, you!" a voice called out.

Mave turned to see a human woman walking toward her with a long pole in her hand. She was dressed in a multicolored sack-dress with a white apron, like the cooks.

"Is that a weapon?" Mave asked. "Please, human, I mean you no harm, no," she said, and her voice sounded strangely high-pitched. Her throat hurt when she spoke, and her hand went to her neck. "Do not be afraid," she whispered. "I am Mave, Queen of Iteria."

The woman's mouth curled into an odd shape, and she pressed her dark eyebrows together. "You lost, there? Where's your momma and daddy, girl?"

Mave stared at her. "Girl?" she repeated. "I am not. I am not..." She looked down at her hands, then at the rest of her body.

What she saw at first frightened her. She had changed. But soon, as she looked at her new long limbs and pale, hairless skin, and as she stroked with fine, delicate hands the now soft hair on her head, she knew what had happened.

"I was too busy seeing this new world to notice the change," she said in a voice that shook. "But of course, yes," she reasoned. "It is the only way for trolls to walk in this world."

She smiled at the human woman who stared back. "Do not be afraid. I am human, yes."

· THIRTY-FIVE ·

"Now what are we going to do?" Annah asked as she and Eelin stole through the corridors. Annah held tight to the sword at her side to keep it from clattering on the floor. The fighting was still going on outside. She was afraid to think of how many Iterian trolls might have been lost to the Duots. "How will we ever get the stone now?" she whispered.

"We must find Mave," Eelin said.

Annah felt a pain in her gut at his words, fearful that finding Mave would be difficult, and thinking of their betrothal at the same time. Would the two of them send me home? she wondered. Just then a troll in full guard uniform bumped into them.

He stared at Annah, then at Eelin. He had a beard that seemed to cover his entire face.

"Have you not seen a human before?" Eelin snapped.

The guard began to back up. "Human. Filled with disease," the guard said.

Annah waved her blade at the guard. "Then you know my blade can slice you to ribbons at my command and fill you with death."

The guard ran off howling.

"I know a secret way out of here," Eelin said. "It's a way that Mars will surely have guarded before we get to it." He grinned. "But you are brave. You will save us both."

Annah and Eelin ran down the corridor and down a stairway that led to the kitchen. "But first," he said, "I am famished and must eat." He grabbed hot bread out of the cook's hands. The cook said nothing, his mouth agape. "Prepare food for our journey," Eelin commanded. "And be quick about it." The cook bowed and went to work.

They gathered everything in sight, filling leather bags. "I am your king," Eelin said, giving the cook a stern glance.

Annah followed Eelin into the stable through a hidden door in the kitchen. Once inside the stable, Eelin climbed a set of rickety stairs that led to a loft. "Be careful," he told Annah.

They stood on a stone platform with a small door at one end. "This is the secret way," Eelin said. "The King's Door." Slowly he crept into a low tunnel that appeared to lead downward. On his knees, he stopped and touched Annah's arm. "Give me that blade," he told her. She did so. "And follow me."

She followed him through the small passageway. At the end of the low hallway was a spiral set of stairs. Annah thought the King's Door was really a passageway that smelled of mold, and of untouched dead things. The stairs opened to a cave with a tunnel at the far end. Eelin motioned for Annah to be quiet as he tiptoed toward the entrance. With outstretched hand, he advanced forward, and was met by a guard with a long saber. The blades met and Annah screamed, covering her mouth.

The guard had never seen a human apparently, for he stopped in midswing to look at Annah. Eelin knocked the guard's sword out of his hand, and pushed him back into the cave.

Annah snatched up the sword. "Now walk," Eelin said, with his blade pushing into the troll's back.

They entered finally a garden at the back of the Hall and circled the lake. Once they had reached the passageway, Eelin let the guard go. "Tell no one what you saw," he commanded.

Below the lake, in the grotto, Eelin and Annah stopped to survey the carnage there. On the ground near the lake lay the bodies of Duots and Iterians both, and there were Hazans too, uniformed members of the king's guard.

Fires burned everywhere. The banner of the Army of Iron, a silk cloth with letters sewed onto it, still flew, held by a soldier of the Army, but not far away was a sea of dead bodies slashed, pinned by lances and bows and axes, faces frozen forever in death's grimace.

"Such waste," Eelin said.

They stood, looking down at the sad ground beneath them. It was as though a hundred fires had blown up from underground. There were piles of dirt and fires the once neat earth was torn and thick with the stain of blood and the smell of death. Even the lake was caked and tinted with blood.

They hurried past the grotto, Eelin holding his side. Under his fingers oozed purplish blood.

"We must take care of that wound," Annah said.

"Later," Eelin answered, pressing his wound harder. "We must get to Iteria without delay."

"What about Fally?" Annah asked, looking back toward the Hall. "I'm afraid..."

"Fally can take care of himself," Eelin replied. "And Modoc is more than brave. We have to reach Mave before..." He didn't finish.

"And what about Mars? Is he dead?" Annah asked.

"I truly doubt it."

ಊಐ

They arrived at Modoc's cavern with barely a word spoken between them. To Annah the journey went swiftly, because they didn't pause to rest, and because the road had grown familiar to her.

Modoc and Graley were glad to see them and attended to Eelin's wounds, sewing up the larger one on his arm while Annah watched. Neither Modoc nor Graley said a word about Jaden and Annah wanted to comfort them but was afraid to say anything. She thought she saw Graley wipe away a tear, but maybe it was just fatigue. Finally when their eyes met she nodded, and Graley nodded back. Annah tried to be thankful that Eelin was all right, so that she wouldn't cry.

"And what about Mars?" Modoc asked, himself wearing a patch across his eye and a large bandage around his hand. They sat eating in the War Room.

"The wound was not mortal," Eelin answered.

"I would have finished it," Modoc said, spearing up a handful of tubers.

Eelin sighed. "I know you would have, Uncle."

"You do what is right with you," Modoc said. "And I do what is right with me."

"Did you lose many?" Eelin asked quietly.

"Not quite half. We were victorious," Modoc said.

"I wonder if Fally survived," Annah said.

"He survived without wound," Modoc replied, touching her sleeve. "At least that is what I was told. We arrived back here only this rotation."

"Do you think the war is over?" Annah asked.

"Not as long as Mars is alive," Modoc said, glancing at Eelin.

"If I get the stone the war will be over," Eelin said. "The humans will come one by one."

"And Mars will kill them one by one," Modoc said. "And where is the stone? Did you get it from Mars?"

"Stolen," Eelin whispered. He shook his head and picked up a handful of tubers and gobbled them down.

"Stolen?" Modoc repeated, his black eyes widening.

Eelin was silent for a moment, as though he was trying to believe it himself. "He said Mave took it."

"And why would she want it?"

"I think I know," Annah said. "The Saqa has the power to make trolls walk in the human world."

"That is a legend I have heard," Modoc said.

"I told Mave about the legend. I learned it from the Chronicler," Annah said. She reached out and took a handful of brown tubers and ate them. She was so hungry they had no taste or smell. She was too tired to eat more, even though her stomach growled terribly.

Eelin watched her as she spoke and ate, shaking his head.

"It is my fault," Annah continued. "I told her what it was like in my world. I think she wanted to go there and see for herself. She was curious."

"And she, in her stubborn way, no doubt figured out how to see it," Eelin said in a confused tone. "She is clever."

Annah watched as Eelin and Modoc looked blankly at each other. "She might have found a book..." Annah began. "<u>The</u> book."

Eelin's hands went to his head. "The book and the seed and the stone." He grimaced. "She found it all…"

Annah shut her eyes. "Oh!"

"Mars showed me Father's book, it was ancient and broken," Eelin said.

"But she can't read," Modoc snorted.

Annah looked sheepishly at Modoc. "I taught her a few things. She wanted desperately to read and I tried to teach her, though I don't think it worked. But she might have learned a word."

"The book had drawings," Eelin said. "I saw them."

"I might be able to find the passageway," Annah volunteered. "I think I might know where she would go with the flower."

"I'll go with you," Modoc said, pounding his fist on the table.

"No," Eelin said, placing his hand on the old man's fist. "You stay here with Graley." He nodded at Annah. "We can take care of this, Uncle. The stone will once again be in my hands, do not worry."

· THIRTY-SIX ·

Annah and Eelin crossed into Iteria exhausted. Although Eelin's wound was well sewn and bandaged, it still oozed blood whenever he used his arm. "You've got to rest your arm," Annah told him, but he wouldn't listen to her. "I'll tie it to your side," she threatened. She had wanted to make him smile, and he had smiled, but she knew he had smiled for her benefit.

They were greeted at the Iterian castle by Fally, looking much older and thinner than he did when Annah had last left him. He hugged them both, and drew them inside. "You have no idea of my joy," he said. "To see you both alive." But within moments his face was bathed in sadness.

"Mave has disappeared," he said. "And I'm terribly concerned about her."

"She has the stone," Eelin said.

"And I'm sure she's gone to make a passageway," Annah finished. "But don't worry," she added.

"But why?" Fally asked.

"She thought she could go through the passageway," Annah said.

"She had everything she wanted here," Fally said. "Why would she leave Iteria?"

"She didn't want to rule as queen," Annah said. "She wanted someone to take care of her. She wanted to stay a child." She paused, surprised how easily she understood Mave now. "She wanted to be me. And," she whispered, "I wanted to be her."

Fally shook his head. "She could die in the human world. Trolls with sight, it may be only legend...."

"That's why we've got to find her quickly," Annah said. "Because we don't know what is legend..."

"And what is truth," Eelin finished.

"Like finding a sliver of glass in a pool of water," Fally said.

"We'll split up," Eelin suggested.

Fally nodded in agreement. "I'll go to the Lime Caverns. It has many small twists and secret rooms. And Win, she will know a few places."

"Good," Eelin said.

"I'll go to the Gallery," Annah volunteered, "because she loved it so."

"I'll go with you, and after that we will go to Great Fork," Eelin said. "I know a cavern where she used to go when she was angry with me."

"You'll rest first, of course," Fally said.

"Where is her chamber?" Eelin asked suddenly. "I want to search for my pouch. The one that contained the seed."

"Just there," Fally said, pointing up the hallway.

༺༻

After a brief rest they ate and within the rotation they left for the Gallery. Annah was silent as she and Eelin rowed down the river toward the City of Glass. She put her hand into the water and let it float there, watching her hand become red-tinted. What if we do find the passageway? she wondered. I'll have to go home.

"I am sorry," Eelin said, rowing through the syrupy water.

Annah didn't speak until the boat was docked and they made their way up the road to the Gallery. She tried to think of the words that would make him change his mind.

Finally she simply spoke the truth: "I have nothing there. Nobody."

"You belong with your own kind."

Annah stopped walking to face Eelin. "Do I seem so different from you?" she asked.

Eelin didn't answer. "Somewhere, in your world, you have parents. Your mother, you found her."

"My dream mother is nothing but that. A dream." She paused. "But you are real."

"You must go back."

"I want to stay here... with you."

"I know."

"We could rule. Together."

Eelin cleared his throat. He turned to face her. His eyes were full of tears. "That is not possible. A human and a troll cannot ever..."

"That's not what I meant," Annah said quickly. But it was what she meant. She wanted to be with him.

Eelin took her by the shoulders. "It is what I meant." He pulled her into his arms and held her, and stroked her hair.

She held onto him with a passion that she had never felt before. Not for anyone, human or troll. "She doesn't love you," Annah whispered.

"Annah, I wish with my soul that we could be together, that we could... but we can't change what we are."

"We don't have to," Annah said, looking into his eyes. She searched his face, wanting desperately to memorize it. His nose, flattish, nostrils flared, the dimple on his fat cheek, and the long tuft of hair at his chin.

"It cannot be. That troll dress you wear will not change you."

"I don't want to go."

"I will make you go." He pushed her hair away from her eyes. "I am ugly, monstrous to you, am I not?"

Annah shook her head violently. "The opposite. To me you are, you are a lion…"

Eelin silenced her with a hand. "There, you see. We are of different... form. I am nothing more than animal to you."

"No, not an animal, a—wild creature," she cried. "Oh, it doesn't matter."

"Can you live in a world where the sky and moon and clouds are shut out?"

"What is there for me at Seton House?" she asked, fighting back tears.

"Where your entire world is a web of caves, molten heat, yet no sun?"

"I can see," Annah said, blinking.

He didn't answer. He took her hand and led her on. They came to the Gallery, and the moment they entered the room Annah knew they had found the place. She felt the magic. She scanned along the ceiling of the cavern. The blue glow on the uppermost book ledge was so slight you would never notice it unless you knew to look, but it was there—the line, fine and perfect, as though someone had taken a blue pencil and drawn it in the air. And the whole room was faintly blue, as though a blue moon had found its way into this room, a human thing, out of place, a human color.

Eelin said, "It is the place. I can feel it, yes."

Annah tugged on his shirt and began to pull him back toward the entrance. "No, it isn't." She wished she'd never suggested the Gallery.

Eelin began to walk around slowly, looking up. He took a deep breath and let it out. "It's here. I felt the same strength when I held the stone in my hand. When I first found you." He looked at her.

Annah felt tears pooling in the corners of her eyes. "I was wrong, it isn't here."

But now Eelin was staring up at a place high up near the roof, on the top book ledge. "There," he said, grinning. He went to get the ladder and rolled it across the room, its wheels screeching like a bird. He positioned the ladder, and held it steady and said, "Now up you go." He pushed her gently.

Annah reluctantly began to climb. The glow of the crystal was there all right. She could see the light clearly and knew that it could see her too, just like it did that day when she fell past it in the toy box passageway.

She reached the top rung and climbed out onto the wooden shelf and plopped down. There, on top of the books, stood a pot where the beautiful scarlet flower grew. Directly above it was the passageway, a perfect circle with light shining down onto the plant.

Eelin climbed up the ladder and sat next to her. "It is a good thing to see," he said, settling next to her.

"Good for you, not for me," Annah said.

"Oh, your doll! And your book!" Eelin cried suddenly.

"I don't need them any more," she muttered. The words surprised her, and were not really what she'd meant to say. "I'll come back for them," she said under her breath. She looked up into the blue crystal and saw her mother's eyes, the same violet blue. "How is it I had to come here to find my mother?" she asked Eelin.

He smiled. "It's magic you found when you came here," he answered. "Though I think you had it inside of you before you came."

Annah wiped her face on the leather sleeve of her dress. She was not aware how fast the tears had been falling. "I promised the Chronicler I'd return, and now..."

"I'll tell her you had important business back home," Eelin said, stroking her arm. "You'll find your mother, I know you will."

Annah smiled bitterly. "I'll find Mave first," she said.

Eelin examined the Saqa flower, and reached up to touch the petals. "The Chronicler spoke the truth," he said. "Look, there is a strange fruit on the plant. I have not seen this before." He twisted his face into thought. "It must be this fruit that allows the sight." He looked straight up through the passageway and then shielded his eyes. "The sunlight is too strong!"

Annah looked at the purple fruit and shook her head. She peered up. "Yes, it's sunlight." She blinked her eyes. "It's the sunlight that makes the fruit grow. There was no sunlight in my passageway." Through her tears she felt the beginning of a smile tugging at her lips. Because she understood the magic at last. The Chronicler did indeed speak the truth.

"And now you must go," Eelin whispered hoarsely. "Then I will take the stone and hide it where nobody will ever find it."

"But what about Mave?"

He shrugged. "I hope she is happy."

"And what about the kingdoms?"

"I will unite the kingdoms, as planned."

"You will rule both kingdoms alone?"

He nodded without looking at her, and she knew he was lying. He would find a troll and marry. And he would forget all about her.

Annah stroked the purple petals. The flower was so beautiful. "I won't ever see you again, will I?"

Eelin didn't answer.

"What will you do after I'm gone?"

"I will do what I am destined to do. Mars must be stopped. Now, go," he said. "Go, and may you..." He looked into her eyes and touched her face. "May you find the truth." He brought his face close to hers, and kissed her lips.

Annah kissed him back, with a passion she had never felt before. She clasped her arms around his waist, not wanting to let go.

He gently pushed her toward the passageway.

Annah touched his bristly cheek for a moment, and then stood up. "I will find a way to come back," she promised, tears streaming down her face. She studied his kind face, then closed her eyes tight, to fix his image forever in her memory. Then she opened her eyes. The sunlight hit the top of her head and she began to stretch herself out toward it. Next to her Eelin's hand took hers, then let go.

She climbed out of the hole and found herself in a field of sunflowers and mustard grass—every shade of yellow imaginable. Kneeling, she peered down into the passageway, and saw the blue light. She let her hand dangle inside.

Eelin took her hand between his warm palms. "Good-bye, Annah, human with a soul. Good-bye," he said, and his voice sounded gravelly and deep, not at all like it did a moment before. "I know you will find her..." and then his voice trailed off and Annah thought he was crying. "Good bye." His voice sounded faraway, like a dream voice.

Annah whispered, "You do love me, don't you?"

Silence.

Annah rose. She stood in a meadow which faced rolling hills, and beyond them, the blue thread of ocean. She began to walk, slowly as though waking from sleep.

She turned to look at the hole from which she had just climbed, to make sure it was still there, to make sure that finding Haza and Eelin had not been just a dream. The ground was tinged in a perfect circle of blue light, the light that led to Eelin.

She turned her back and ran as fast as she could away from it.

· THIRTY-SEVEN ·

Eelin sat on the shelf for a long time after Annah had gone. "So far away," he said, looking at the Gallery below. "And yet so close to the other world." He knew he should take the crystal from the flower, climb down, and make his way back to Haza. Instead, he found himself staring into the crystal, hoping it would help him. He was frightened.

"Do not forget me, Annah," he whispered, squinting up at the sunlight that flooded the Way. He shielded his eyes as they began to burn.

"What is wrong with me?" he asked. "First Mave, and now Annah." Never had he felt so alone and so confused. "If only Jaden were still alive. He would know what to do."

He touched the fruit of the Saqa. The purple fruit smelled like nothing he had smelled before, as rare and wonderful as humans themselves. Would it really let him walk, let him see in the human world?

And what of his life in this world? "Am I truly destined to rule both kingdoms alone?" he asked, looking around at the Gallery books for an answer. "What of the prophecy?" He laughed bitterly. "It will never be. The Iterians will never let me rule without an Iterian counterpart. The Hazans, yes, but not the Iterians." He would have to marry an Iterian. He thought about his life's journey so far, reminded himself of his purpose. To sit on the Chair of Light as king over two clans united. To possess the stone and create passageways and let humankind come freely through the Way. To keep Mars from bringing death to the troll race.

None of that seemed important now.

"This Way will not be discovered for a thousand ages," he whispered, trying to convince himself that he could leave it be and come back to it. Escape to it.

He touched the warm crystal, the last crystal. He should have been happy, now that he had the stone, but he wasn't. The desire to be king was slowly leaving his body like blood draining from a wound. Part of him was missing. There was no order to his life without—what was it? Was it Mave? Was Mave even alive? "She glimmers like a jewel in my memory, though she never cared for me," he whispered. "Or at least, she never let on."

He felt terribly weary. He closed his eyes and leaned against the wall. "Sleep brings wisdom," he whispered. But he couldn't sleep. There were too many unanswered questions.

"What is my destiny?" he asked, tugging at his braids. The thought burned in his soul. "It is not my place to question the gods," he reasoned. "My duty I have always known: to be king. But first I must take the Chair." He looked down at the ladder that led back to Haza and the Chair, and to war with his own flesh and blood.

Then his eye turned to the purple fruit. "And what is the Truth?" He reached into his pocket and took out the strand of Annah's hair he had found in the leather pouch when he searched Mave's chamber. Tied with gold thread, it was his only connection to Annah. She probably didn't even know it existed. Or perhaps she had left it for him as a gesture of kindness or perhaps pity. Pity. He prayed that wasn't the reason.

He smiled and stroked the hair across his cheek. "Annah. We are bound by all that we are, and all that we are not. I should not have let you go." He closed his eyes to see her face. "Yes," he whispered. "In answer to your question, I do love you. Love you, yes."

He shook his head in an attempt to clear his mind. "Is that my duty? Has my life underground been in preparation for the life I am to live above?"

He knew the answer even before he plucked the fruit.

He took a bite of the fruit and the sweet juice, even as it flowed down his throat, warmed him to his toes.

The moment he swallowed the first morsel, he began to change. With each breath he grew taller. His waist-length hair grew fine, his bones thinned, and his skin became smooth of hair. The skin was rust brown, all one color.

He touched his limbs, and gasped at the change in his body. "I am human," he said in a trembling voice. "So this is how it will be."

On the flower fruit had sprouted, holding the magic of a thousand lifetimes, allowing him to see in the human world.

He stood upright on the bookshelf and pushed his head through the passageway. He looked up at the human sky. He looked, and his eyes and skin drank in the heat and light. The feeling made him dizzy, made him smile, and brought tears to his eyes, now closed.

He climbed through the passageway, his bare feet pushing into rocky cavern sides, and then into soft human soil.

He stood up in the new world and gazed around. The sun was more magnificent than he could ever have imagined. As he watched, the sun changed from yellow to red-orange as it began to skid down the sky. It hovered, shimmering, on the horizon and he realized that it was setting. "Squii," he said, in the ancient tongue.

Open-eyed, he took in these, the human colors he had longed to see. He took a deep gulp of the mild, flower-sweet air and said a prayer to the gods to give him courage as he passed into this new age of wisdom, perhaps the true age of wisdom.

He began to walk, tall and straight, through the yellow flowers, feeling their downy heads brush his open palms, and the powdery dirt caress the soles of his feet.

He walked toward the emerald hills and the sunset that was, as he always knew it would be, the exact color of Annah's hair.

The End

Made in the USA
Columbia, SC
17 July 2021